HOT & BOTHERED

HOT & BOTHERED

Short Short Fiction on Lesbian Desire

Edited by
KAREN X. TULCHINSKY

ARSENAL PULP PRESS
Vancouver

ARSENAL PULP PRESS
103-1014 Homer Street
Vancouver, B.C.
Canada V6B 2W9

The publisher gratefully acknowledges the assistance of the Canada Council for the Arts for its publishing programme, as well as the assistance of the Book Publishers Industry Development Program, and the B.C. Arts Council.

Typeset by the Vancouver Desktop Publishing Centre
Author photo by Dianne Whelan
Printed and bound in Canada

CANADIAN CATALOGUING IN PUBLICATION DATA:
Main entry under title:
Hot & bothered

ISBN 1-55152-051-6
1. Lesbians' writing. 2. Lesbians—Fiction. I. Tulchinsky, Karen X.
II. Title: Hot and bothered.
PN6120.92.L47H67 1998 808.83'108353 C98-910079-0

Acknowledgements

A huge thank you to Lawrence Schimel, who conceived of the idea of *Hot & Bothered* and its companion book, *Quickies*.

Thanks to:

Brian Lam and Blaine Kyllo of Arsenal Pulp Press for making this book happen (and for continuing to publish gay, lesbian, feminist, politically left, alternative culture, and other great books).

James Johnstone for tons of support and assistance.

Victoria Chan and Richard Banner for helping me with millions of computer nightmares.

Dianne Whelan for the gorgeous cover photography. Ruby and Alex, the models.

Val Speidel for the fabulous cover design.

Sandra Fellner, postie extraordinaire who, through snow and sleet and wind and hail, cheerfully delivered buckets of mail.

My friends, family, mentors, and supporters: Arlene Tully, Lois Fine, Tova Fox, Maike Engelbrecht, Mark MacDonald, Lisa McArthur, Dix, Judy Newman, Jess Wells, Nisa Donnelly, Rachel Pepper, Charlie Tulchinsky-Hamazaki, and Trigger.

My beautiful and charming fiancée, Terrie Akemi Hamazaki, for love, support, encouragement, and for keeping me constantly hot and bothered.

And to all the great writers who contributed hot and bothersome stories.

For Terrie:
the woman who makes me hot and bothered

Contents

Introduction

First there was The Kiss. Roseanne and Mariel Hemingway. Remember what a fuss it caused? Then there was The Other Kiss. Judy Davis and Glenn Close. Same fuss. Same boring kiss. Then Ellen came out. Every dyke bar in North America had an Ellen Coming Out party. If only such celebration occurred every time a dyke came out. On the other hand, it *was* a cause for celebration. The main character on a prime-time television sitcom declares she's a lesbian. Break out the champagne. I guess we have come a long way since Miss Jane Hathaway of *The Beverly Hillbillies* was the only lesbian (sort of) on TV (unless you want to count Alice from *The Brady Bunch*).

When I was growing up, lesbians on TV, in movies, or in magazines were virtually non-existent. The music world was ruled by heterosexual men and the occasional heterosexual woman. I remember how affirming it was for me to read lesbian fiction when I was first coming out. It was a hard time in my life. The world was opening up and I was discovering my love and desire for other women. At the same time, all kinds of doors were closing in my face. I was painfully aware of my difference. As a teenage bar-dyke in the late seventies, I figured if people hated me for being queer, it was my own fault. My burden to carry. Homophobia was a word I had not yet heard. One thing that helped me through this difficult time was books: books about dykes, about our attractions to each other, sex with each other, and relationships. I lived in a big city with a growing lesbian community. I can only guess how crucial these books might have been to dykes who lived in small towns and rural areas.

Hot & Bothered is a book about lesbian desire. Some of the stories are passionate, others are hilarious. Some are sad, others are sexy. By "desire" I don't mean only erotica; in fact some of the stories don't have any sex in them. What the stories have in common is the theme of women's desire for other women, which is just as important to write about in 1997 as it was in 1967, when lesbians were just beginning to publish fiction about their lives. One need look no further than the popularity of Ellen's on-air coming out to notice how starved dykes are for media representations of themselves.

In *Hot & Bothered* I include sixty-nine stories from a variety of voices. The authors range in age from their early twenties to late sixties. There are contributors from Australia, Canada, England, Israel, Mexico, South Africa, the United States, and even Bulgaria. Their stories are about seduction, betrayal, aliens, tattoos, sex in nature, sex with a real estate agent, butch-femme attractions; fantasies about a boss, a co-worker, a saleslady, a fellow diner in a restaurant, a high school teacher, a passenger on the subway. There is sex at the office, sex on the phone, a public piercing, a lesbian vampire, there is sweet romantic love-making between long-term lovers, hot, anonymous sex between strangers, unrequited love in the convent, loving a lesbian mom, lesbians in the lingerie department, a woman in love with her dildo, and a sexual tryst with the lovely Ms. Marge Simpson. Most of the pieces are contemporary, and there is an excerpt from Elana Dykewomon's *Beyond the Pale*, which takes place circa 1912. Some of the stories will make you hot. Others will make you bothered. Some will do both.

The stories in *Hot & Bothered* are short. Snapshot fiction. A taste, a bite, a stolen glance when the beautiful woman across the room is not looking; a one-night stand, a quick look. These are bedtime stories, fiction to get your best girl hot, fantasies to read over the phone to your long-distance lover, tales to enjoy on your own in a steaming bath, behind closed doors, or on the bus on your way to work. Short and sweet. Quick and rough.

In these short works of fiction, the authors will delight, seduce, amuse, and move you. Sex is so personal, so subjective. What one woman loves, another fears; what one woman craves, another dislikes. Just as it takes all kinds of cars to fill the highway, it takes all kinds of dykes to make a community. This book represents the wide spectrum of dyke experience. I invite you to sit back, pour yourself a glass of wine, or a cup of herbal tea, open the book and enjoy.

—Karen X. Tulchinsky
Vancouver, B.C.
January, 1998

S A R A H   S C H U L M A N

People in Trouble

IT WAS THE BEGINNING OF THE END of the world but not everyone noticed right away. Some people were dying. Some people were busy. Some people were cleaning their houses while the war movie played on television.

The cigarette in the mouth of the woman behind the register was cemented with purple lipstick. She had lipstick smeared on her smock. Tiny caterpillars of grey ash decorated the sticky glass countertop.

"I'll take these two," Kate told her, holding each bra in a different hand.

"You'd better try them on," the clerk answered with a quick professional assessment. "These are too big for you, miss, and after a certain age you can't count on growing any more in that direction."

"They're not for me," Kate said, enjoying herself thoroughly. "Cash, please."

Which one would Molly wear first? She held them in her hands, absentmindedly running the material through her fingers. Kate would see them on Molly's body before she touched them in place. There was the demure lace that opened from the front, like walking in through a garden gate. Then there was the really dirty push-up that didn't need to open. Kate could lift Molly's breasts right out over the top. Kate held them in her hands. She could run her fingers over the lace and feel its texture as she felt Molly's nipples changing underneath.

"Leopard-print crotchless panties on sale," the woman added, folding ashes into the wrapping paper. "Maybe your friend would like a pair of these, too. Great with skirts."

It would be three days before she saw Molly again. Kate climbed the stairs to her lover's apartment and left the package by the front door with a private note.

When they did meet on schedule, Kate felt a certain nervous eroticism wondering which one Molly had chosen, which one was waiting for her under Molly's soft blouse.

"You're sexy," Kate told her at dusk. "You have languid eyes and beautiful breasts. I gift wrap them as a present to myself. Your breasts are beautiful, creamy, and sweet."

She pressed her hands from Molly's face to her chest and felt the shape of the lace underneath, but then kept going back to that wisp waist and the sloping shelf at the end of her back.

"But it's your ass that turns me on tonight. Tonight it's your ass that's hot."

Then she thought, Am I really saying these things?

Molly pulled her out of the early streetlight and into a shadow, so the gypsy reading fortunes in the storefront across the way wouldn't have to push her kids into the back room out of sight. Molly arched her ass, sliding over Kate's flesh so that Kate felt her lover's warm body against her chest and the cool brick wall on her back.

"Let's go up on your roof," Kate said.

"You really want to do it, don't you?" Molly laughed, her neck smelling like cucumber.

"Guess so."

"Let's go," Molly said, looking sparkly and quite lovely. "Besides, there's not that much time left."

There was a change, then, to a quiet happiness and a certain sense of contentment that accompanied them up the stairs. On top of the building there was only heaven and a radio rising from illuminated shapes. A man was smoking somewhere—they could hear him cough. The radio was a thin reed. There was a child to the right and silverware clattering, all below. There were undiscernible cars, frequently, and a chime and a voice.

C E C I L I A   T A N

Love's Year

IT BEGAN IN APRIL, because she said that was when she began, and it was a time for new things. She taught me more than one new thing, like how to kiss her and fondle her at the same time without fumbling either one. She said my kiss resurrected her, and hers made me bloom. In May we discovered sex out of doors, long hours in the rope hammock, each with one of the other's hands tucked between our legs, until we were both satisfied and the Goddess had played tic tac toe upon our backs. But our moment in the sun was yet to come. June was a month of true summer, when I learned to lick the sweat from her back, when we would soak the sheets with our wetness, so slick we were like seals or mermaids as we slid against each other. The intensity of July sent us to the mountains, to laze in a cabin by the lakeshore, but by evening when the mosquitoes came out, we would have already spent the afternoon biting one another. By August the heat became too much for me and I struggled to hold her at arms length. But I was too torpid to move that fast, as she licked at me like I was ice cream. With September came first day classroom feelings as she sensed my unease and began to instruct me in new endeavours, how to hold her gently afterward, what to talk about when the sweating and sucking is over. In October she declared it the season for indoor sports, and so I held her like a bowling ball, thumb in one hole, fingers in the other, and she ping ponged me from wistful to wanton and back again.

November was the month of the turkey baster.

Snow came in December, and long mornings spent in bed after office closings, her hand sliding between the blanket and my stomach, her hair around her head like a wreath on the pillow, but somehow I knew her heart was no longer a gift. January we celebrated with a kiss at midnight, but it would be a winter of discontent. By February the cold was bitter. And in March that is exactly what I did.

L U C Y   J A N E   B L E D S O E

A Desert Night

THE STRING OF SEVEN LIGHTS, bobbing ever so slightly in the night sky, changed their course. They had been moving in a line perpendicular to us, toward the mountain range in the distance. As we stood and watched, utterly naked save for our flip-flops, the lead light turned slowly, imperceptibly at first but by now decidedly, and headed directly for us. There was something else: I had the sense, the strong sense, as did my friend when we talked about it later, that these bobbing lights were guided by intelligence. They headed for us, as if to sniff us as an animal would do, moving neither randomly nor by a prearranged pattern or blueprint—without precision and *with* decided will. They seemed curious.

As they approached us, my fear intensified. In fact, I had never been more frightened in my life. Not when I developed early signs of hypothermia while skiing in a white-out. Not the time I clung to the edge of a crumbling cliff, looking down hundreds of feet below me. Not when I stood alone for the first time in my new place, a room that was vomit green and maybe eight feet square, after leaving home at eighteen. While experiencing these earlier fears, I somehow had remained engaged. I had known I couldn't indulge the fear, because I had to act.

This time there was no action to be taken. The seven bobbing lights were approaching, dipping lower in the sky as if to get a better look at the two naked women in flip-flops. Yes, I admit I did go so far as to imagine some form of spacecraft landing, of a hatch opening, of little beings waddling toward me. Pointing. Laughing. Forcing me into their spacecraft. Explaining in perfect English, or in garbled alienese, that they wanted me for science experiments, or worse, on their planet.

I did imagine abduction. In detail. And for those moments I truly believed it was possible.

Begging my friend to come with me, I began to run. Where do you run to in the desert? It was irrational, of course. There was nowhere to go but back to camp. At least that was a home of sorts and I needed to get there. As I ran, panting, I looked over my shoulder. The lights kept coming, bobbing, taking their time, while I, a naked bundle of human cells, ran through the desert night. I quit looking over my shoulder and just ran.

In hindsight, I'm glad she tackled me, though if I'd been a few years older I'm sure she would have induced a heart attack. My scream seared the cooling desert air. The impact of her body knocked me face first in the sand, silencing the scream and restructuring my fear. Like the way an injection of energy can transform the molecular structure of a substance, the skeleton of my fear, though still fear, took on a powerful erotic charge. I was grateful for the length of my body against the earth. And for the length of her body against mine.

She apologized for the attack from the rear.

"Don't move," I said. The pressure of her body relieved my loneliness, wholly.

It was not, she explained, that she was any less scared than me, but her fear had taken another form. My running terrified her, made her feel we'd provoke a chase, like running from a bear.

We lay in the sand together, our bodies wet and gritty with perspiration plus sand, our gasping the only sound for miles. The lights, still in a line, oscillated in the not far distance but seemed to have stopped their approach. As if they'd seen enough of these pitiful earth creatures, they turned, again imperceptibly at first, and headed for the mountain range. We watched them retreat as we made love, voyeurs to the aliens, their menace feeding our passion. Eventually, the first light rose slightly and skimmed over the peaks, then dropped behind the mountains, out of sight. The rest of the lights followed, one by one, each rising to miss the peaks, and disappeared behind the range. Then, feeling equally foolish and anointed, somehow favoured, we talked hungrily, the human voice an oasis. We tried to imagine the bobbing lights being piloted by American soldiers in green camouflage suits, running surveillance or tests or simply joyriding in some new, or not-so-new, toys. With the military, we agreed, anything was possible.

But that was just the point: anything *was* possible. And as we talked, the military explanation seemed just a wee bit more absurd than other possibilities. The idea that only this one planet, only this one speck in the universe, sponsors intelligence is illogical. Think of the ant making a journey across my friend's hip as we lay in the desert sand. I am sure that it, along with all its comrade ants, perceived itself to be the top rung in the order of things, entirely oblivious to the existence of humans and most other species, even though by some remote chance this one was traversing a human body as we spoke. Isn't it possible, even likely, that we are the ants to other forms of life or intelligence in the universe? Couldn't we be just as oblivious?

My friend brushed away the ant and rose to her knees. She walked on them to a nearby succulent I couldn't identify. She weaved her fingers among the thorns in order to grasp a fat leaf, tore it from the plant, then crawled back to me. She broke off one of the thorns and used it to trace the tattoo on my breast. Then she dug her fingernails into the flesh of the leaf, accidentally piercing her palm with a thorn, and cursed. Still she continued until she managed to break the rubbery flesh. A clear gel oozed out. She scooped a fingerful and applied it to my skin, cool and slippery.

As I relinquished myself once again to her hands, I realized that all of us—the bobbing lights, whether military or alien, the ant traveling the landscape of my friend's body, and even I—were on reconnaissance missions. Hadn't I come to the desert to watch, to see, to measure myself against what I found here? We are nothing but this watchfulness, this constant reconnaissance, in the hopes of finding fertile geography on which to feast, whether that geography be a piece of fruit, a person, a desert, a planet. What matters is the simultaneous feast, being laid bare, the sand in your crevices, the sting of the agave leaf, tattoo needle or starlight, the place where your flesh intersects another geography. I closed my eyes to better concentrate on the sand scraping against my back, the something sharp—a piece of rock or a thorn—digging into my hip. In my left ear I heard the tiny clatter of a hard-shelled animal, and on my skin, the balm of her mouth and saliva, fingers, and cactus pulp.

DOROTHY ALLISON

Her Thighs

I WAS THINKING ABOUT BOBBY, remembering her sitting, smoking, squint-eyed, and me looking down at the way her thighs shaped in her jeans. I have always loved women in blue jeans, worn jeans, worn particularly in that way that makes the inseam fray, and Bobby's seams had that fine white sheen that only comes after long restless evenings spent jiggling one's thighs one against the other, the other against the bar stool.

After a year as my sometimes lover, Bobby's nerves were wearing as thin as her seams. She always seemed to be looking to the other women in the bar, checking out their eyes to see if, in fact, they thought her as pussy-whipped as she thought herself, for the way she could not seem to finally settle me down to playing the wife I was supposed to be. Bobby was a wild-eyed woman, proud of her fame for running women ragged—all the women who had fallen in love with her and followed her around long after she had lost all interest in them. Hanging out at softball games on lazy spring afternoons, Bobby would look over at me tossing my head and talking to some other woman and grind her thighs together in impatience. The woman was as profoundly uncomfortable with my sexual desire as my determined independence. But nothing so disturbed her as the idea other people could see both in the way I tossed my hair, swung my hips, and would not always come when she called. Bobby believed lust was a trashy lower-class impulse, and she so wanted to be nothing like that. It meant the one tool she could have used to control me was the very one she could not let herself use.

Oh, Bobby loved to fuck me. Bobby loved to beat my ass, but it bothered her that we both enjoyed it so much. Early on in our relationship, she established a pattern of having me over for the evening and strictly enforcing a rule against sex outside the bedroom. Bobby wanted dinner—preferably Greek or Chinese take-out—and at least two hours of television. Then there had to be a bath, bath powder, and toothbrushing, though she knew I preferred her unbathed and gritty, tasting of the tequila she sipped through dinner. I was not supposed to touch her until we entered the sanctuary of her bedroom, that bedroom lit only by the arc lamp in the alley outside. Only in that darkness could I bite and scratch and call her name. Only in that darkness would Bobby let herself open to passion.

Let me set the scene for you, me in my hunger for her great strong hands and perfect thighs, and her in her deliberate disregard. When feeling particularly cruel, Bobby would even insist on doing her full twenty-minute workout while I lay on the bed tearing at the sheets with my nails. I was young, unsure of myself, and so I put up with it, sometimes even enjoyed it, though what I truly wanted was her in a rage, under spotlights in a stadium, fucking to the cadence of a lesbian rock-and-roll band.

But it was years ago, and if I was too aggressive, she wouldn't let me touch her. So I waited, and watched her, and calculated. I'd start my efforts on the couch, finding excuses to play with her thighs. Rolling joints and reaching over to drop a few shreds on her lap, I scrambled for every leaf on her jeans.

"Don't want to waste any," I told her, and licked my fingers to catch the fine grains that caught in her seams. I progressed to stroking her crotch. "For the grass," I said, going on to her inseam, her knees, the backs of her thighs.

"Perhaps some slipped under here, honey. Let me see."

I got her used to the feel of my hands legitimately wandering, while her eyes never left the TV screen. I got her used to the heat of my palms, the slight scent of the sweat on my upper lip, the firm pressure of my wrists sliding past her hips. I was as calculated as any woman who knows what she wants, but I cannot tell you what magic I used to finally get her to sit still for me going down on my knees and licking that denim.

It wasn't through begging. Bobby recognized begging as a sexual practice, therefore to be discouraged outside the darkened bedroom. I didn't wrestle her for it. That, too, was allowed only in the bedroom. Bobby was the perfect withholding butch, I tell you, so I played the perfect compromising femme. I think what finally got to her was the tears.

Keeping my hands on her, I stared at her thighs intently until she started that sawing motion—crossing and recrossing her legs. My impudence made her want to grab and shake me, but that, too, might have been sex, so she couldn't. Bobby shifted and cleared her throat and watched me while I kept my mouth open slightly and stared intently at the exact spot where I wanted to put my tongue. My eyes were full of moisture. I imagined touching the denim above her labia with my lips. I saw it so clearly, her taste and texture were full in my mouth. I got wet and wetter. Bobby kept shifting on the couch. I felt my cheeks dampen and heard myself making soft moaning noises—like a young child in great hunger. That strong, dark musk odor rose between us, the smell that comes up from my cunt when I am swollen and wet from my clit to my asshole.

Bobby smelled it. She looked at my face, and her cheeks turned the brightest pink. I felt momentarily like a snake who has finally trapped a rabbit. Caught like that, on the living room couch, all her rules were momentarily suspended. Bobby held herself perfectly still, except for one moment when she put her blunt fingers on my left cheek. I leaned over and licked delicately at the seam on first the left and then the right inner thigh. Her couch was one of those swollen chintz monsters, and my nose would bump the fabric each time I moved from right to left. I kept bumping it, moving steadily, persistently, not touching her with any other part of my body except my tongue. Under her jeans, her muscles rippled and strained as if she were holding off a great response or reaching for one. I felt an extraordinary power. I had her. I knew absolutely that I was in control.

Oh, but it was control at a cost, of course, or I would be there still. I could hold her only by calculation, indirection, distraction. It was dear, that cost, and too dangerous. I had to keep a distance in my head, an icy control on my desire to lose control. I wanted to lay the whole length of my tongue on her, to dribble over my chin, to flatten my cheeks to that fabric and shake my head on her seams like a dog on a fine white bone. But that would have been too real, too raw. Bobby would never have sat still for that. I held her by the unreality of my hunger, my slow nibbling civilized tongue.

Oh, Bobby loved that part of it, like she loved her chintz sofa, the antique armoire with the fold-down shelf she used for a desk, the carefully balanced display of appropriate liquors she never touched—unlike the bottles on the kitchen shelves she emptied and replaced weekly. Bobby loved the aura of acceptability, the possibility of finally being bourgeois, civilized, and respectable.

I was the uncivilized thing in Bobby's life, reminding her of the taste of hunger, the remembered stink of her mother's sweat, her own desire. I became sex for her. I held it in me, in the push of my thighs against hers when she finally grabbed me and dragged me off into the citadel of her bedroom. I held myself up, back and off her. I did what I had to do to get her, to get myself what we both wanted. But what a price we paid for what I did.

What I did.

What I was.

What I do.

What I am.

I paid a high price to become who I am. Her contempt, her terror, were the least of it. My contempt, my terror, took over my life, because they were the first things I felt when I looked at myself, until I became unable to see my true self at all. "You're an animal," she used to say to me, in the dark with her teeth against my thigh, and I believed her, growled back at her, and swallowed all the poison she could pour into my soul.

Now I sit and think about Bobby's thighs, her legs opening in the dark where no one could see, certainly not herself. My own legs opening. That was so long ago and far away, but not so far as she finally ran when she could not stand it anymore, when the lust I made her feel got too wild, too uncivilized, too dangerous. Now I think about what I did.

What I did.

What I was.

What I do.

What I am.

"Sex." I told her. "I will be sex for you."

Never asked, "You. What will you be for me?"

Now I make sure to ask. I keep Bobby in mind when I stare at women's thighs. I finger my seams, flash my teeth, and put it right out there.

"You. What will you let yourself be for me?"

E L A N A   D Y K E W O M O N

Beyond the Pale

FROM OUR MAKESHIFT TENT, Rose and I could see the occasional shape of a girl walking by. We lay in the night heat listening. Branches and dry leaves crackled as they were added to late cooking fires. Laughter, bits of song and discussion floated on the humid air. A layer of perspiration enclosed me like a sticky soap bubble, making me feel that no matter how much I wanted to touch Rose, she'd find me unappealing. A firefly flew inside our sheet-wall. I watched it try to find its way out again, blinking through the shadows. Rose took my hand.

"No one will bother us here," she said.

"I'm covered with sweat."

She licked my arm slowly. "Yes,"she said, "salty."

"I don't smell bad?"

"You smell better than dinner to a laid-off seamstress."

A light breeze came up the cliffs from the river and dried my arm where her tongue had been, giving me a shiver. I leaned up on my side and looked at her. There was just enough light from the moon and the camp lanterns to see by. Her hair was pinned up off her neck and I could make out the small mole below her ear. She was wearing her lightest cotton slip, twisted tight across the mound of her belly.

Sometimes her body seemed as far away as the moon when I watched her cleaning up on Essex Street or coming out of work with her friends. But tonight the moonlight was in the river and I could dip my hand in and drink it if I dared.

"Maybe I don't smell so good to you?" she asked. Her eyes, which had echoed the July sky all day, were grey in the dark. Even so I could see, now that I was looking at her body, her confidence leak away. I put my nose close to her armpit.

"You smell like the plum orchards of Bessarabia."

"You're a liar."

"You accuse me, your own cousin, of lying?" I poked her side lightly and she poked me back.

"At the very least, a flatterer," she said, pressing her hand against my arm.

"I know what I smell, and you smell delicious." I put my face under her breasts, resting on the upward curve of her stomach. In fact, we both smelled sweaty and smoky. How she really smelled was familiar and strange at the same time, the smell of a freshly bound leather folio, compelling.

"Rose—"

"Yes?"

I turned my face up to look at her. "Would you take your slip off?"

She looked at me intently and we both sat up. All these years, we'd never lain naked together. We'd hardly seen each other's bodies unclothed except for the few seconds between pulling off our skirts and putting on our nightgowns, and when we let our towels loosen in the baths. I could feel a stone poking my thigh through the featherbed. I didn't care. From a few directions I could hear soft moans but no footsteps.

Rose heard the moans too and smiled. "Yes," she said as she pulled the slip over her arms. She folded it neatly. "Now you."

I peeled mine off and used it to wipe the sweat from my face before I threw it in the corner. Sitting, Rose's flesh made a generous fold above her belly. I slid my hand under the fold and squeezed her flesh upward lightly. Rose's eyelids trembled, her lips parted as an "aaah" crept up her throat, and then she opened her eyes wide, as if she were frightened.

"Rose," I said, leaning close to her ear, "you are my heart's desire."

"Flatterer," she mumbled into my cheek, relaxing as she kissed me.

Then we were prone again, naked on our bedrolls. And scared. Strangers surrounded us. Yet we were also beyond fear—the shop girl's camp was like a wall protecting us against our ordinary tenement life. I loved her softness, the resiliency of her flesh when I pressed my palm into it, the way a mossy riverbank springs back from your step. I rolled over on her body.

"I'm not too heavy like this?" I could feel the pressure of my chest flattening her breasts.

"No, you feel good."

We were sweating so profusely that I slid against her. I swayed into that sliding sensation, holding myself up on my wrists, back and forth, my small breasts tickling the pillowy surface of hers. We giggled when I guided my nipple exactly onto her nipple, and they both puckered, taking on the shape of ancient towers. I started to rock, my thighs slipping up and down hers. She pushed her belly up hard into mine and rocked with me.

"Put your whole weight on me again," she whispered.

I fell into her mouth, grabbing her thighs for balance. We kissed and swayed, slipping. My feet tilted off her calves and curled back around her toes. Between my thighs the sweat gave way to a different stickiness and behind my shut eyes a bright green flashed, seesawing my focus between mouths and lower limbs. Our legs tightened together, straining into each other, as if we wanted to get beneath the thin cover of our skins or melt the skin together, like candle wax. In a corner of my mind I could see the *havdale* candles I made as a child, felt my hands braiding the warm wax while it was pliant, two wicks intertwining, mingling with the sharp smell of the spicebox.

I opened my eyes to watch her face as she filled, moving beyond self-consciousness, moving with me. I arched to let one hand move between our bodies, supporting myself on my other arm. Rose seemed to hold her breath. I rubbed the curly hair below her belly, tugging it lightly until she gasped, and opened her eyes.

"Anything,"she breathed, "anything you want."

"Anything you want," I echoed with the same urgency, "—everything." I turned my hand sideways, holding the fingers tightly together and entered the folds of her as I might slice through the uncut leaves of a book. I closed my eyes again, listening. Rose was taking short, hungry breaths and I could find the rhythm of her breathing in the pulse I felt coming up through her inside lips. I turned my hand again so that two fingers stroked her small mound. We called it the inner nipple, since it grew larger and harder when we excited each other and seemed connected to our other nipples by an invisible thread of flame. Rose grabbed my arm. Her grip was strong from years of sewing and carrying, and I felt almost faint from the pressure, from flooding. Rose was moaning and for the first time I didn't feel a need to shush her. I heard myself groan as I slipped the two fingers deep inside her and she tightened her muscles around me, clasping me as I shook and pumped.

For a moment Rose seemed to stop breathing altogether. Her muscles grabbed my fingers tight and her hips strained upward from the featherbed while her head rolled back. Then she gave a cry and jerked, gasping for air, relaxing and then squeezing my fingers and crying out a second, a third time. I felt my interior muscles contracting with hers, and cried out too. Then she collapsed in on herself.

Her laughter surprised me. At home she often pushed a pillow over her head when we got this far, to stifle any noise. I pulled my hand out. A thin film made a web between my thumb and forefinger. I held it to my nose and sniffed, smiling at her strong smell, which carried a faint scent of the herring we'd eaten for dinner.

She took my hand and put it to her lips, kissing my fingers. "You are a blessing, Chava, my blessing."

Far away I heard another girl laughing—because of listening to us or her own pleasure? I rolled back onto my side, wiping my hand on the bottom sheet of our makeshift tent. Then I lay in her arm, nuzzling her breast slowly. What a pleasure to be naked. Rose stroked my hair, murmuring deep in her throat.

"And you?" she asked after awhile.

"I'm completely satisfied," I said.

"Completely?" she asked, moving her fingers down to the hair of my vee.

"Completely," I said, stopping her exploration. All I wanted was to lie there in the calm, feeling the liquid surface of my skin suffused with her body.

MARIA DE LOS RIOS

The Language of Pain

At a leisurely pace, my right hand slides inside the black leather glove. My pupils fixate on Alina's fat, naked body partially wrapped in black satin. She waves one hand in the air to the beat of Celia Cruz, *"Dame yierba Santa pa' la garganta."* The other hand turns the pages of *La Mala Vida.* I face her thinking of Kahlo's self-portrait, "The Broken Column," where her bound and surgically wounded torso is painted tall and breathtaking. My fears, my pain, plastered in hues of indigo, are pushed into eloquent silence behind a crevice of memory on that tempered bruised canvas that is my soul.

Alina's irreverent thick lips command, *"Nena, sácame la mugre."* The way her juicy lips part as she speaks, her skewed grin, double wide ass, full breast, those dangerous curves of her bodyscape, bring images from the past. The backyard where round, ripe, and sweet mangas pulled down the mango tree branches. Those mangas swung back and forth, rubbed their nipples against the dry orange dirt. In my mind, the image of her two girls, Nina and Y'te ame, slapping against my face invoke flashes of those days back in my hometown when I used to bang a manga against a flat rock, squeeze it between my hands until it got ready, ripe, and juicy. My lips would bite its scratched nipple and suck its pulp until rivers of sweet warm juice overflowed my mouth.

Now, I find Alina more enticing than mangas. Still, I want to bang her against the flat bed, squeeze her between my hands until she gets ready, ripe, and juicy, scratch her nipples against the cold granite, bite them. I want to suck her pulp until rivers of bitter, sweet, hot juice pour out the sides of my mouth.

The lamp's switch turns. An action followed by a reaction brings back a shimmering sight. The candle in her altar comes back to life. While my ungloved hand holds the leather wrist with a tight grip, black fingers sidewind like snakes, eager to strike and deliver. She pants, yearns, burns.

I peel the sheet wrap, contemplate her landscape, slowly crawl to her on four legs. With my ass up in the air like a wild cat, I nuzzle her. She gasps, grunts, moans. The leather hand slides from her feet up to her crotch. It parks between her thighs. She resists. My free hand comes to the rescue, and soon, she is wide open. I delight in the glitter of Alina's wet, swollen pussy.

Her dark folds release a strong spicy scent. In my mind, I anticipate their tangy flavour, bite my lower lip and survey the vast terrain in front of me. There is so much land to explore. I hesitate. Where to begin? I stare, detail. Promptly, my leather hand glides over her topography, registers every feature with cartographic precision. The way I look at her makes her wet. The way she gets wet, makes me hard.

She hands me the candle. I cast a circle of wax over her rib cage. She quivers in ecstasy. I sense her tremors slowly increase in magnitude. Her sea floor spreads. I recede. My eyes scan changes in her swollen folds as they thrust. Her fingers follow a strong impulse. I snatch her wrist, move her hand away. *"Nena, nena . . . "* she begs. I ebb. She flows.

She looks into my eyes, wets her lips in a way that makes Orinoco flow between my legs. My leather palm circles Nina. She thunders. I clip Y'te ame between my fingers, wet it, stroke it, bite, chew, suck. Both nipples stand tall.

My rough paw descends in slow motion, presses her skin like *cunaguaro* claws. It trespasses highlands and lowlands. It reaches wet margins, dives into her waters, pushing in, sliding out, swimming in circles around and about. I work out her pouch, stretch her elastic walls, play in and out, go deeper and deeper. Soon my entire hand dips in. *"¿Cómo sabes nena?"* she roars. I keep on diving. She keeps on burning, receiving my electric strokes, seismic intensity. *"Nena, que rica eres,"* she grunts. My fist pumps with Caribbean rhythm. Her hot ring of fire catches my wrist.

Abruptly, the possibility of this being the last time hits me. The knot in my throat builds. I want to cry, but instead, I keep pumping deeper and deeper, stronger and stronger. It's not love that runs in my veins now. It is rage. Why? Why her? From all the women in the world, why Alina? I push with fury, as if I have the power to change the course of events, control the future, erase her cancer.

She brings me back to the moment, "tell me, how do you know?" I look into her eyes. They overflow. "*Sigue, sigue* . . . don't stop," she whispers softly. I can't play this game when I feel so vulnerable, so fragile. All my heart desires is to hold her in my arms and cry with her. I stay there immobile, lost in the dusk of timelessness. Her hot margins expand and contract sucking me in.

I take a deep breath, rest my face against her leg, pump my fire to her depths, shake her body, shape, form. Measure her lust, curves, waves, strength, passion. Provoke her action and reaction. Bang with intermittent strokes. She explodes with the force of an earthquake. I feel her inner contractions, her aftershocks. Her margins tight around my wrist, hold me in. I lay over that familiar body, so much a part of me, feel her heat. I am so scared. What would life be like without you, *compañera?* She gives birth to my hand.

GERRY GOMEZ PEARLBERG

Unfinished Tattoo

IT WAS THREE A.M. and I was sound asleep when the doorbell rang. The candles in my room had almost melted down. It was dangerous, I knew, to doze in a room full of burning candles, but there seemed no other condition under which to wait for her.

She wore eyeshadow and lipstick. A brown leather jacket. In her hand, a large paper bag. For the moment it took me to unlock the front gate, she lingered on the threshold of my stoop, part of her still belonging to the street where desires linger unfulfilled, and part of her almost within my grasp. I relished the moment of that transition, of locking the door behind her, pocketing the key, and turning to kiss the evening, that other world, from her lips.

When she came in, my dog knew exactly what it meant. He greeted her briefly, then scampered up the stairs to wait for us at the foot of the bed. He knew where we were headed and that we always went directly there.

In my room she said, "I have a request." She asked me to cut her clothing off with my knife, the one with the iridescent white pearl handle. It had once belonged to a famous star, a very famous star, a singer; I won't say her name because you wouldn't believe me anyway. The blade was blunt, so it took awhile to slice away her dress, her slip, her fishnet stockings. It was more like sawing than slicing which gave things a refreshing, amateurish tinge. I pressed my blue-jeaned knee against her mound. The slow, insistent sound of slashing cloth was like rain hitting the window: suspenseful and energizing but also somewhat sad. We were enraptured with the leisurely near-violence of it.

When all her clothing lay in tatters on the floor, only the delicate gold chain with the sacred heart of Jesus adorned her body. That, and the half-finished tattoo on her inner thigh. It was a tattoo she had started—a small blue serpent—but had given up on when the pain of the needle's repeated penetrations became too great. Something to do with accumulation of pressure, she said. Her thigh bore the coiled tail of a rattlesnake, half realized, whose front portion appeared to have slithered into her very flesh, or been absorbed by it, or simply slipped into a realm beyond that of skin and bone. I was fascinated with this unfinished tattoo. It meant the world to me.

Back then, I thought she was so beautiful. Now, eons later, though we no longer speak, I still do. I don't exactly want her again; what I want is even more improbable: to revisit that night with her, to remain in it as if it were a room. I want the sound of her satin slip rending apart while her blue lipsticked lips spread wide. For her to say to me again, "My mouth is a sex organ." For the glint of candlelight, a knife blade, her dark, dark eyes, the ninth orgasm, and the sacred heart of Christ, that glorious, damaged metaphor. For rain the way it used to be when water was still free. For those first roiling sensations of love in spite of all the evidence—hard and soft—against it.

In her nakedness, she eagerly undressed me. Everything but my belt fell to the floor: that she kept close at hand. Nude and kneeling, we held each other for a long time, breathing not speaking, our pubic hair sparking.

Finally, she opened the paper bag she'd brought with her from the Metropolis. A rectangular Styrofoam container lay inside. She opened it like a jewelry box and the candlelight glancing against the assortment of sushi seemed nearly divine. It transformed the deep red tuna into slabs of velveteen, soft steps to an ultimately unattainable altar. It illuminated the ginger slices like shards of stained glass the colour of pink dogwood blossoms. It made the wasabi gleam like clubmoss, and the scaly black-green nori almost translucent, at once stiff and yielding, a half-snake coiled in its den.

"Where I come from," she whispered, "when a woman is attracted to someone, she feeds them with her fingers."

She lifted a piece of yellowfin sushi, rubbed it lightly against the wasabi bulge, dipped it in the small plastic cup of soy sauce, and put it to my lips. We went on like that all night, fucking and feeding each other and playing with my belt, and with the chopsticks, experimenting with the wasabi's steamy insinuations on mucous membranes. The room smelled like ginger, horseradish, salt—mouth-watering and clean.

In the morning I awoke to gelatinous fish roe in the sheets. I looked for her but she was gone. Something to do with the accumulation of pressure, I suppose.

I still come upon remnants of roe from time to time when cleaning behind my bed. They have somehow retained their ruby-like sheen, though desiccated now, weightless, and harder.

DENISE NICO LETO

On This Land Under Water

I CRAWL OUT OF BED, not fully awake yet, and careen gently toward a light in my lover's room. I have on a long, deep green t-shirt and my dark hair is in a soft state of chaos around my head. She is at her desk working. She looks up and smiles. There is expectation, wonder. I move closer. My breasts graze her face. She looks at them slowly and with patient appreciation. Her eyes are full and wet: blue fish, idle fins. Everything is soft and slow, as if we were under water and could breathe. And it is not that time stands still, it is just that time is of no consequence.

The possibility of staying under water so beautiful, without the usual equipment, for as long as it takes, is what our love is like.

She runs her hands up my sides, the small of my back, along my hips, lightly across my breasts which suddenly become awake and my whole body sighs and gives way to this motion. She is breathing slower to account for all the heavy, soft water around us. I am quiet, my breath a steady current. Her hands move down my hips to my ass. She pulls my pale green, cotton underwear down little by little, peaks in, strokes the top of my pelvic bone, lets out a long, low moan like a heated animal searching for shade. She picks me up and in one movement we are on the bed. Her mouth is on my nipple. A hard, round, purple mound. It looks like candy which she licks and bites and plays with, until it grows and is so sweet, I laugh and yell and beg her to take it, finally, completely.

The unhindered home of our bodies together. The luminescence, the spell of that liquid beauty where breath and sound and need are one.

Everything is different now, focussed. She straps on the dildo. The sun coming in from the window seems thick. I can see dust particles floating in a ray of light. Her short brown hair is sticking up, her body its own kind of lever lifting me, my entire body on top of her. She places the dildo against my belly, then moves it slowly between my legs, lets the hardness rest on my pussy awhile. We say nothing. In the silence there is my body taking her in; taking her in my body. What matters is the angle, the depth of light through streams of sweat, the curve of our bodies against the sheets, the silhouette. She slides the rest of the dildo in, exquisitely, just so. She runs her hands down the curve of my hip, my ass. She moves harder and faster. I am open and opening. I grab the covers, moan something that becomes an incantation: over and over again I moan. She pushes, grabs my ass, slaps it lightly. My incantation exceeds all reason. She slaps my ass, pushes the dildo in, slaps, pushes. Her hands are pressed hard on my back, and she is fucking me and I am open and full. We are like this for so long the slant of light shifts, the rhythm pulls and we change forever: breathing under water, as if that was what we were born to do.

But, looking in on this, the world is smug and collapses easily on the assumption that what was real here was that which was most readily seen: the tiny bubbles on the surface.

She turns me over, lays me down on my back, unstraps the dildo from her body, leaves it in mine, licks the bright curl of my clit, pulsing, swollen. She takes me in her mouth, all the while going in and out, in and out. Our sweat is a beautiful faucet, a testimony of this whole new tundra of water and I come so strong she does not have time to witness the first ripple, the slow tensing of muscles—just the fierce immediacy of my concentrated pleasure, my scream of love, my whisper against the silence.

And that is what they come to hate. The tiny bubbles like claw marks on the glass surface of propriety. Irritating sign-posts of what rumbles underneath. But we know different. The deeper terrain is always the more dangerous. Lesbian sex in the time of the fathers is always submerged and subversive.

We lay in bed together. My naked body leaning into hers, swaying comfortably, slowly. We have no need to come up for such air as that. We can breathe on this land under water and how.

S U S A N   M.   B E A V E R

By the Water

LAKE SEDUCES ME UNDER THE CLOUDLESS SKY. I sit down on fallen tree, close to her wide, round body, and stare into her. The lake, she stares back at me: bold, unabashed. As she flows and moves, as her surface undulates and refocuses the sun into a hundred more suns, her waves reach out to me and I reach out to her. Drawn down and in to the darkness I can feel the pull on my cunt rising through my body and into my fingertips. I reach out and her chill shocks me. Withdraw, she's too strong for me, but I lick my fingers. I can smell the lake on them. Footsteps crunch the sand behind me.

"The lake reminds me of breasts." I turn to look at her, shading my eyes with my hand. A raven flies out of the sun behind her. "Fluid and free, don't you think?" she asks. I nod. She seems to rise from the grey mountains behind her, towering over them. Raven laughs. "Go ahead," he seems to say, then laughs again.

"I want to jump in," I say. "But she's kind of cold." The sun hurts my eyes, so I stare into the lake again.

"It's only because your skin is so hot," she says. She walks around me and I can see her brown skin and wide owlish cheekbones. Her hand moves toward my face and draws a leaf from my long hair.

My lips are salty. Her hand drifts down my arm until she reaches my wet fingers. Her mouth is hot around two of my fingers. "Come with me," she says and an eagle screams high in the mountain behind me. I turn to look, but she pulls my head back gently. "Swim," she says, then presses my fingertips to her neck. Closing my eyes I can feel her heart beat and I remember round dances at powwow time. When I look at her again I feel my grandparents with me. I wonder what my aunties are doing right now. Are they sitting under maple trees telling stories about the way the reserve was before roads and electricity? She's laughing and pulling off her clothes. I keep looking at her as I slide my t-shirt over my hard nipples and she follows my hand as I draw my shorts over my hips. Her eyes rest on my thighs.

The water wakes my whole body at once. I don't think I can comprehend the sensation. There's supposed to be a fish as old as these hills, so I keep my eyes open. So clear I can see all around me, except to the bottom. There's a hand on my thigh and I roll in the water to face her. She's smiling and reminds me of the coyote who once played a trick on me in my dreams. Before I can move closer she kicks to the surface and I follow, drawing my tongue up her thighs, through her triangle of curly black hair and up her belly. I hold her breasts as I surface and she licks the water from my cheeks, my lips. This is what it feels like to be touched. The sky is open and wide between two mountain ranges. Down here in the valley, I feel small, but I know I'm growing out of the lake, past the mountain tops up to where Eagle tells the Creator our prayers. If I reach out Eagle will brush me with her wings.

A brown bear stops and drinks at the edge of the lake.

This smiling coyote woman draws me to the shallows and stands with her thigh between my legs. I rock in the water as though riding a mare through a rain storm. Cedar. I can smell cedar. Sweet. Beyond the mountains behind me I can hear a rattlesnake shifting under his shady rock.

I can't stop until I hit the sun and inhale yellow light. This is what it feels like now. I am a feather falling from the sky.

I want her. I push her toward the bank and as she lies down in the sand; I bury my tongue in her dark, dark lips between her legs. Faster, then, I put my fingers inside. She shouts, or maybe it was Eagle again.

Pine trees sway and moan in the breeze, then it is quiet. Even the wind has calmed her breath. I can see Bear moving through the tall grasses and sagebrush away from us. Just over this smiling woman's shoulders the sagebrush waves and tickles the air. The woman, now laughing in my arms, smells like her cunt and the richness of the lake. When I look back to her, I see eyes darker than the mountains reflected in this very lake at night. But the light that shines from her is like the rippling sun on the lake. She's seductive, drawing me down, and in.

K. LINDA KIVI

Moonriders

WHEN THE MOON CAME UP over the hill beyond the pasture, it glowed like a round eye looking for the places we call home. My home, your home—why, I wondered, leaning over the sill of your grandmother's bedroom window into the salty lavender breeze, could we not have found *our* home beneath this shared sky?

It was there, in your grandmother's bedroom, as the moon came up, that you slipped your fingers inside of me from behind. I gasped, nearly lost my grip on the wooden sill, almost pitched through the gaping windows into the garden of poppies and forgotten mint below. I pulled your fingers inside of me, held you tight in my depth, felt the warming of nearly forgotten places. I was glad your grandmother was gone; I didn't have to stop myself from crowing to the cows who, warm and content, had chosen to moonbathe in the fragrant French night.

There was clover in the air, a touch of Mediterranean salt on my tongue, and we smelled of passion, of the juices you beckoned by the pulse of your hand. I wanted to hold on, I wanted to let go, I wanted to turn around and throw you onto the fat feather bed that we had just risen from. I wanted to roll in your juices, smear mine across your cheeks and belly, lose myself in the folds, fill the entire house with the song of that creaking bed.

Bed song, my song, I chanted a litany of yesses to you that night, one yes tripping over the next, drawing you further and deeper into me, making the world forget that we had chosen to part, chosen the familiar past over the promises of passion that drew us together. I hung onto the window sill as though it were possibility itself.

When was it that you threw me back onto our symphonic bed? That you took me in mouth and hand, and tore the remaining furrows from my brow? My openness amplified, grew loud and enormous, until I was moon-sized and radiant. I grew until I was so large I could see everywhere in those hills of your grandmother's, of your childhood. Everywhere.

I saw the bolete mushrooms, as big as our furled fists, pushing up out of the needle-carpeted forest floor. Below the surface of the gleaming pond, where one lone cow had gone to low at the ripples, I felt fish nibble on secretive toes. In the vineyard, I plucked the grape-laden vines and covered you in purple juice.

Oh take me.

S'il te plaît, s'il te plaît.

Take me again.

Like you did so many times. On the fat slab of kitchen table that is of a wood so old no one remembers its tree, the salt shaker and pepper grinder clamouring as we rocked to all four seasons of Vivaldi. In the train, your face buried under the veil of my skirt, while stony towns and wind-tipped cypresses parted the way. While dancing barefoot across the dark wooden floors of your grandmother's house, Cointreau and butter-soaked Breton crêpes leaving trails around us.

I want to be that me again.

Like I was.

Love me harder, deeper. The breeze and the ghosts of your grandmother's house urged me on, opened the armoire doors and snuck out to watch our pleasure. The unmarked but pungent bottles on the dresser uncorked themselves and their sweetness spread like elixir. That was the night the moon stole me from our singing bed. I was drawn out as if my skin had disappeared and I faced the night with my bare, bare flesh fully exposed.

You fucked me so well. "*La lune! La lune!*" I cried out when I came and you didn't miss a beat. Only the cows paused to watch the madwoman who had come to live in your grandmother's house.

Later, we lit the fireplace in the faded kitchen, we roasted onions in the coals. You fed them to me layer by layer, pulling each one back, one at a time. There are no tears in a cooked onion, you said, only sweetness and a caramel tinge where the embers have touched hot. Because you could not keep me from rubbing the soft, warm onion flesh all over you, over the mound of your belly, your buttocks, your calves, we ran the bath.

That house of your grandmother's has a tub with the taps in the middle, as though it were designed for love. But whose? Your grandmother's? Or ours? We climbed in, leaned back, played with each other's nipples and labia with our steamy pink toes.

And the bowl of dried rose petals on the shelf above the tub made a gift for us. The parched red petals flowered again when they touched the hot water. They spread, opened, even seemed to find their true colours. One lone petal floated while the others sank. It crossed the momentarily still waters. Where would it go? Would it sink too?

I am drawn to you, my fine French lover. But the ocean is such a tremendous tub, too large, too cold, too rough to let the petals fly and float, even if the same moon shines on both sides.

Come, I wanted to say, but left with only a kiss and more memories.

So, I'll say it now. I'll say it here between these lines of passion and love.

Come to *my* grandmother's house.

Come to Turtle Island where bears and deer nibble on wild purple berries and coyotes ride the moon. Come here to the heart of cedar forests where the snow falls so gently that the winter hare leaves its trail across my yard. I can hear the pileated woodpecker calling, knocking and calling and knocking again. It is your turn now, your turn to take wing and find me in my home.

Let fly, *ma cherie*, let fly.

SUSAN FOX ROGERS

Naming

IT'S THE FIRST DAY OF CLASS and I'm having my students write the story of their names. They like to write about themselves, to tell who they are and where they come from. They are eager, and good, and so very young. When they are done I will remember their names. Stories make me remember.

I write with my students, I am one of them, exploring language and writing. So I must write, but I am tired of writing the story of my name. What I want to write about is my other names, your other names, names we give or take.

Sam is what I call you, a name given to you by friends when you wore a Sam Spade hat, cool and slick. I could see the Sam in you even before I knew your name, even when you told me it was Louise and I knew that that was wrong. Who named you Louise?

Sam is the name I call you when I am in bed with you, when I am calling out, "Oh God, Oh Sam," as if Sam and God are maybe the same person.

I have not given you any names, as I have with lovers past, you are not pumpkin or orphan girl or kit-kat. I have not endeared you in this way. Or distanced you.

The only other name I attach to you is Bob. And only when he is attached to you. Bob, the big brown cock, complete with balls, came named. Bob was my birthday gift from you. I told you I wanted a cock just for us. "Good thing I'm not really a boy," you said. And I laughed. Good in many ways.

I like the name Bob. It's a solid name, not too serious. But only I know that about him, and you.

Cocks are named. The boys I knew liked to name their cocks. There was skinny Tim with his enormous dick. "Let's name it Spike!" he said. He adored Spike. I did not.

You have other cocks, and they do not have names, but they have stories. They tell of where they have been and who they have seen, like my students here, writing the stories of their lives. I can hear the stories just by watching.

With my first woman lover, we named our cunts. To have a cock was unthinkable. Mine was Twyla and she had a life of her own, was a newborn aching for attention. And my lover named hers Miranda. Such lesbian names. I would call her from my corporate job and ask: how is Miranda today? and she would say: difficult, out of control, can you come get her? and I would laugh and go back to typing a memo. We thought we were so clever.

And now you have a name for me, but the time for this writing assignment is up, and I must find something to read to these eighteen-year-olds who have written about being John Russell Jr. and Melissa Smith, so full of the history they are sure is flowing through their veins.

"Let's finish," I say. I panic because I cannot read to them of cunts and cocks, of Sam and Bob, of Twyla and Miranda. And I wonder if I will ever tell the story I want to tell.

"Who wants to read first?" I ask. A silence descends. I let it sit. I have learned to wait. I am a student of language and writing and I will wait to tell the story of the name you have given me.

GABRIELLE GLANCY

S & M

ALL MY GIRLFRIENDS' NAMES, without exception, have begun with S or M. It was not until Sasha, however, that I had my first official S/M relationship. When I tell you the circumstances, the frustration, the attraction, the particular curve of her particular elusiveness, you will perhaps want to hit her too.

We were in Brooklyn, sleeping in the living room of her friends Linda and Lani's brownstone. Linda and Lani were a warm, wealthy lesbian-activist couple who were trying to have a baby. She had not picked me up from the airport. True, she was waiting for me, but she had made me suffer.

Stiff at first—it had been three months since we had seen each other—Sasha got up from the couch and put on music. Of course, she played the tape she had sent me from Moscow. I began to cry. Then when she got into bed, I fucked her in the ass. I had two fingers of one hand up her ass and two fingers of the other in her cunt. I could feel the thin wall that separated one from the other, slick, hot between my fingers. I fucked her good and hard. She was on her stomach. I stood over her. When she came, I thought she would cry. I myself was exhausted. I rolled over next to her.

For a long while we lay without talking. Then I said: "That was really good for me. I like fucking you in the ass. Was it good for you?"

"It was great," she said. "But you know what I really wanted?"

"What?"

"When you were back there?"

"Yeah?"

"I wanted you to spank me."

I felt dizzy with desire.

"To spank you?"

"Yeah," she said.

"With my hand?"

"Yeah."

We were both breathing heavily.

"To fuck you and spank you?"

"Yeah."

"Jesus."

You can imagine what happened the next night.

"Turn over," I said.

Sasha obeyed.

"Spread your legs."

She was wet to the touch, her lips silky.

I found her asshole. I ran my index finger around the edge of it.

"Does that feel good?" I asked.

"Mmm," she moaned.

"Do you want me to fuck you in the ass?"

"Mmm."

"Do you want me to spank you?"

She gasped.

"You do, don't you?"

I ran the palm of my right hand over the smooth curve of her cheeks, the middle finger of my left hand still up her ass. Sasha had a beautiful round butt, small, but beautifully shaped, solid, supple, inviting.

I touched her with delight and calculation. I was about to do something I had only dreamed of and I was plotting my course.

If she had turned her head at that moment, she would have seen my left hand halfway up her ass and my right hand poised in the air, ready to strike.

The preparation lasted a good ten minutes. What I was about to do was momentous. It was a boundary I wasn't so sure I wanted to cross, not because it disgusted me or because I felt it was morally wrong, but because I had the feeling if I crossed it I could never go back. All my life this act had existed only in fantasy. To make it real, to embody this fantasy, terrified me. It was as if in allowing my imagination to find physical form, it would spring loose entirely. I might completely lose control, say everything on my mind, or worse, do everything I had ever fantasized about.

I took my fingers out of her and held the small of her back firmly down, steadying it. Sasha squirmed in marvelous anticipation.

"I'm going to spank you," I said, breaking the silence.

"Do it," she ordered.

She was breathing heavily, could barely speak.

"You want it?"

"I want it."

"Say what you want."

"I want you to spank me really hard."

I couldn't hold back a sigh.

"Go ahead," she said. "Punish me."

The rest is like a dream. When the boundary between fantasy and reality is broken, the world collapses into a moment the size of a dime.

I spanked Sasha red. My hand stung with the blows.

And all the while I was saying something. Without words, I was trying to get her to understand: all the while in the breath of my heart, screaming its awful whisper, back behind the light-spill, I called her. As if to spell it out, with each stroke I gave her, over and over, I was saying: Now! Now do you understand me?

L I N D A   S M U K L E R

Cock

IS IT THE LENGTH? the width? that it grows out of cunt flesh? gives only pleasure and takes so little back for itself? is it the veins which might or might not be there? the constant engorgement? the ejaculation which really happens and soaks our bed? is it waking with desire from which you escaped this morning dressed before I woke? is it the feel of you beneath me my legs straddling your belly? is it the way I torture your nipples without yet being inside you? is it the pull of you against me? legs flailing below my ass unable to move? is it the fact of me shaved head strong jawed? the fact of a woman with a cock an impossibility a reality a presence a challenge a cornerstone? I walked the world today black shirt black jeans and took a passport photo for you I looked and saw myself beside you taller than I am hard-muscled I am that dream and I am that with you the slight hairs on my lip and chin the fact that I can be turned shamed a little boy with a little cock or a little girl with no cock at all told so by her mother and exposed by her father all of that is there ready to come ready to be put on taken off torn from my cunt so my lips can be with you cock my cock mutable the world my world inside of you

L A U R A   P A N T E R

Lobster Moon

BUTTER. GLISTENING ON YOUR CHIN and elbows: your fingers, those eloquent fingers grip the ends of the claw, your mouth partly open, saturated with juice and flesh and sea. Intent on the act, you look occasionally at me, grinning, your teeth and gums ripe with colour. Carefully flipping the lobster onto its back, exposing the small tendrils on its white belly you twist with your fingers, that same delicate movement I have felt on my nipples, and the memory makes me lean forward and kiss you. Sliding a sweet morsel into my mouth with your tongue, you pull back and bite my lip, enough to sting; a punishment for diverting attention from your feast.

Campgrounds have been empty straight across Quebec, abandoned by tourists as the September chill casts itself upon the east coast. Further back, toward the road, scattered campers bearing plates from Wyoming, Arkansas, and California hum with television monotony. We have been driving as if to escape something; glancing backwards, tensing with anticipation. I want to forget the harrowing city, the stench and furor and heavy hearts. This patch of land, perched on the coast of New Brunswick; you blowing softly on lit newsprint and twigs; this is ours tonight.

The fire lights your teeth and jaw, your shoulders obscured by flickering shadows, as if thousands of tiny beings are bouncing around us, teasing our instincts until our arms bat at darkness and our eyes strain to catch a glimpse. When the wind picks up we move closer to the fire, and you pull my hips into your back for protection from the cold. I look over your shoulder, the ocean somewhere beyond us, the white peaks of the waves captured by flames as they wrap themselves around the wood with such passion and persistence, falling back toward the stones and then leaping up, smothering the bark with light. The coals seethe with exquisite beauty; a seductive beckoning to reach out and touch them.

You lean over me, dripping butter and garlic onto my shirt and hair, three of your fingers pushing into my mouth with the last morsel of lobster between them. As I begin sucking you refuse to release it, my tongue lapping at fluid; probing the flesh. You draw the piece back out; my senses strain with longing; and you swirl the white meat again in the pot, your fingers coated with oil and heat. My head tilted back as you place the lobster on my tongue. You watch intently as I savour this gift, my eyes shut while you stroke my neck and shoulders. The liquid on my skin burning with heat from the fire.

I surrender. My desires change forever as the full moon bursts into view, surging over the trees in some victorious gesture: that same movement, night after night. Some unspoken volition turning the circle, the sun and the moon more constant than human devotion. The rays stream over our bodies, the fire diminished in their power. My journey clarified, in that light, by your hands balancing the lobster, its meaty flesh and fluid in my mouth, your body pressed to mine. All paths will lead me here, with the motion of your shoulder, and the shadow it casts; my lips closing over your fingers. This instant, clear as a field bathed in moonlight. The taste as I swallow rich as some precious part of you. I have been opened. Kicking and struggling with uncertainty and regret, I was brought here. The lobster and the moon like a beacon. There is nothing chasing me now.

TERRIE HAMAZAKI

Are You Mine?

WE HAVE MET BEFORE, you and I. In a place far away. In a time marked by turmoil. You, a handsome knight, flashing steel, coat of armour. Come courting for my hand, slaying dragons, brave soldier. Claimed my love as your prize. Breast swollen with pride, heart full of desire, hands aching with lust. Crowned in passion, we wed, my prince and your princess.

Connected to my soul, I seek you out in my present. Feline on the prowl, hungry for her mate. Find out if she's ready. Find out if she's wanting. Find out if she's single. I ask a close friend to spy on my behalf. This butch works fast. Gathers information vital to a Femme's hot pursuit. Phone number, marital status, favourite beverage. This same friend coaches me on my phone techniques.

"Call her up, but don't answer the phone if it rings, let her leave a message," she says. "Go slowly . . . pique her interest . . . and don't forget to change your answering machine tape. Put a Prince song on it. I hear she likes Prince."

"But I don't have any Prince music," I moan. I trust this friend.

"I do," she assures me. "I'll make a tape and drop it off to you tomorrow . . . don't worry . . . you've got lots of time."

You are quick to respond to my initial call. I wonder if you've caught the lyrics of "When Doves Cry" so strategically placed on my machine.

"She called me back," I tell my friend later that week.

"Did she leave a bumbling message like I said she would?"

"Yeah, she repeated her number four times. I'm going to phone her back tonight."

"Call her tomorrow," she says. "You don't want to look overeager."

Yes I do.

I call and you pick up on the third ring. Taking several deep breaths, I ask you out on a date.

You honour the Femme that is me. Tell me I'm gorgeous. Look at me with lust and growing desire. Growl deep in your throat when I push up against you. Moan softly when I nuzzle your neck and stroke your handsome face. I feel protective of you. I feel protected by you. Strolling hand in hand down the street, I am not aware of the flirtations of men directed at me. I don't want it. I don't ask for it. My attentions are solely focused on you. Are you hungry? Are you happy? Are you tired? Are you mine? You smile at me, grin that familiar grin and ask me the same questions. We tease each other, play with each other. Forgetting, just for the moment, the battleground we live in.

You honour the Femme that is me. Tell me, "I do it for you." Try to peek down my top. Rub my black lacy bra against your cheek. Ask me to keep my garter and stockings on when we tumble into bed. Suck hard on my nipples. Want to please me, pleasure me, 'til I scream out my ecstasy.

You honour the Femme that is me. I open my legs to you in conscious vulnerability. I open my legs to you knowing that I want this. I want you. To take me. To make love to me. To fuck me.

You honour the Femme that is me. Call me baby-girl, sweetheart, your mistress, your wife. Let my red-tipped nails claw your back when I come. Hold me tight when I cry. Keep me safe. Keep me warm. I trust you, my butch lover. To not take advantage of your Femme. To understand that my dignity and honour is paramount to the survival of our relationship. And I need you to know that I respect you. That I cherish and adore you. For daring to be butch. For daring to be who you are. Mine.

RED JORDAN AROBATEAU

The Sorrow of the Madonna

SONNY WAS A STREET HUSTLER from way back. She had a bad reputation, which followed her from gay bar to gay bar, even as she moved to escape her own evil comeback in virulent gossip.

I'm still young, but I'm old before my time because of my experience. Because of Sonny, that hard-core butch who was my lover back in '71. She's in here tonight. That hard dyke over there shooting pool? That's her. Sonny—if she isn't calling herself something else by now. I fell for her myself once, bad. She's rugged. But she can be a real gentleman. She has naturally curly hair because her mother's Puerto Rican. If she ever tries to talk to you, get away quick. Just politely pick up your drink and move on down the bar. Stay away from her. She's poison.

The first night I met her I was with my best girlfriend in a women's bar, the Wild Side West on Broadway. She'd worked her way in with us, buying us drinks. Soon she was sitting on a barstool between us, with one arm wrapped around my best girlfriend's shoulders, feeling my leg with her other hand, and keeping up a pleasant conversation. She told us she was lonely and looking for a lover. We were wild and young and had been drinking. We felt loose. My girlfriend slow-danced with her and discovered a secret.

"Guess what? She's wearing one of those strap-on dildos," my girlfriend whispered to me on her return from the dance floor.

Sonny asked if she could take us home. We both said, "Yes," each of us trying to look cuter than the other, competing. "Either one of us. You can choose," we said, alternatively, flirting, batting our eyelashes. "Which one do you like best?"

She said she'd take both of us home. Said she'd paid for a motel room and might as well use it. Cost eighty-nine dollars a night, which was a lot back then. So we went. It was nice. Sonny had her suitcases, suits and a row of men's shoes in the closet. She had femmy ladies' underwear spilling out of the drawers.

She stood in the middle of the motel room, spread her legs in a threatening stance, unzipped her fly, reached in and grabbed a big, purple dick attached to her body under her shorts with a harness. She yanked it out and waved it at us, pounding the rubber cockhead in the palm of her hand. She began yelling orders.

"I'm the boss," she said. "You see this dick? It means I'm the boss. Ya got new names now. Slut and Bitch. Take off your dresses."

She stomped over to the bureau, ripped open the drawers and pulled out some flimsy garments. She threw my girlfriend a black lace teddy and a lacy garter belt for her stockings. I got a red satin bustier, with pink fringe, like a showgirl.

She stripped off my best girlfriend's blouse, but instead of removing her bra, she yanked the straps down off her shoulders and pulled each tit out over her bra so that they poked up, her hardened nipples at attention, pointing straight ahead. Sonny threw the lacy black teddy over her torso and hiked it up around her waist so it showed her pubic hair and her pink pussy.

Then she fucked my best girlfriend, right in front of me. I was so embarrassed. I was forced to smell the pure scent of her gash, hot wet pussy meat, as it filled the room while Sonny was going down on her, ferociously, her mouth full of cunt, getting her ready to take her dick. Then Sonny stood up, stomped over to the chair, grabbed her trousers, and pulled the belt out of its loops. She marched back and wrapped the belt around my best girlfriend's waist, buckled it, and threw her on the bed, face down. As she slammed her dick into my best girlfriend, she gripped the belt in one hand. She fucked my girlfriend from the rear like a rodeo cowboy on a bucking bronco.

Sonny heaved on top of my best girlfriend while keeping her hold on the belt to maintain her grip, because their skin was getting lathered with sweat, slipping and sliding. Her thighs slammed against my best girlfriend's ass cheeks as she drove her dick into her cunt again and again, her clit bumping against it so she orgasmed too. They hollered and moaned, and I wondered, "What about me? Am I just going to lay here? A pretty face, just for show?"

Sonny must have read my mind. She gazed at me with liquid brown eyes and, panting, she said, "Don't feel neglected. I always save the best for last." Then she pulled her dick out of my best girlfriend's pussy, dismounted and crawled over the bed toward me, settled her knees between my legs, spread my thighs open, fingered my pussy with her strong fingers, then mounted me.

She put her purple dick all the way in. God, it felt good. My first dyke to do it that way. The others had just held one in their hands to fuck me, or used fingers. Sonny was so advanced.

We spent five hours in that motel. I came seven times, my best girlfriend eight. Then we had to leave. The phone rang and suddenly Sonny was in a big hurry to get us out of there, running around picking up all traces of us, muttering something to the effect of, "I ain't gonna share my girlies with nobody, since I ain't made up my mind which one I'm choosing yet." I figured it was her old lady coming home.

KAREN X. TULCHINSKY

Famous Last Words

WHEN I CAME OUT IN THE LATE SEVENTIES, butch and femme were politically incorrect. Feminism was in. Flannel shirts were in. Khaki shorts, Birkenstocks, and hairy legs were in. Make-up was out. High heels and ties were symbols of the patriarchy. Butches and femmes were being pushed out of the women's movement. Coffee houses, rape crisis centres, and women's bars were filling up with overall-covered lesbian feminists. Folk music reigned supreme. Holly Near was God.

In 1981, I was a butch looking for femmes in a sea of androgyny. There was only one thing to do. I took to falling for straight women.

Cecile LaRoche was my first. I met her at a fag bar on Yonge Street, a small place that had been there for years. On weekends they had drag shows and a live deejay. The rest of the time customers pumped quarters into the juke box. Tired old queens, pretty young men, working girls, and all kinds of dykes drank beer, met with friends and searched for someone new. One Tuesday night I was sitting at the bar on a high stool when a woman in her mid-twenties walked in and sat down beside me. She ordered a double Manhattan on the rocks, and when her drink was in front of her she pulled out a cigarette and turned to me.

"Got a light, honey?"

I looked into her eyes. Deep sea green, wide and inviting. I fumbled in my pocket for a match. As I held the flame up to her cigarette she touched my hand.

"Thanks, sugar." She slipped off her trenchcoat. She was wearing a short black dress with a plunging neck line. Her large breasts were half-covered, exposing one of the most beautiful cleavages my young eyes had ever seen. Luring me to her apartment was easy. I went willingly for a night of passionate, furious, feverish sex.

As we entered the dark apartment, she pushed me up against the closed door and jammed a stocking-covered thigh between my legs, hungrily devouring my mouth in hard, wanting kisses. I ran a hand up her thigh and under her dress, undoing her garters with trembling fingers. Her hot breath flooded my ear as we dropped to the living room floor.

At five in the morning, she woke me from a deep sleep.

"Come on, sugar. Rise and shine. You have to go now. My husband'll be back in the morning."

"Husband!" I shot upright.

"Yeah, baby. He's on a business trip. But he might be back early. So best be on your way."

I was out on the street within five minutes. "Shit! I knew it was too good to be true. Damn straight women," I grumbled to myself as I walked home to shower and change before work. After that, I put her out of my mind and went about my life, working in the day, going out with friends and searching for a lover in the evenings. One night, about two months later, Cecile was in the bar again. I ignored her, but eventually she came over to me and sat down. She pulled out a cigarette and held it out, waiting for me to light it. I reached in my pocket for a match.

"Come on, sugar. Don't be mad."

I turned away.

"Come on, Bobby. We had a good time, didn't we?"

I shrugged.

"I didn't ask you to marry me that night, if you recall. I asked you to come home and fuck me."

I turned back to her. "Why didn't you tell me you had a husband?"

She shrugged. "I didn't think you'd come with me if you knew."

"Oh."

"He's away again. Won't be back 'til Wednesday." She put my hand on her left breast. I groaned. My breath quickened instantly—I was twenty-one and my hormones were raging. "Please, baby."

I grabbed my jacket, and her hand, and rushed her to the door.

For the next six months we met every other Tuesday. It was always the same. I'd swear to myself it was over, she'd come along and seduce me. I'd cave in and we'd go to her place and fuck all over the apartment, our passion a runaway train heading for the edge of a cliff, momentum building to a fiery crescendo. Skin against skin, lips and tongue, blood collecting in swollen clits and raw nipples. Dangerous sex. Impulsive, voracious, out-of-this-world sex. The kind you read about in trashy novels, born of power and passion and impending peril.

Then, before dawn, I'd wake from exhausted sleep, throw on my clothes and she'd kick me out, teasing me with tongue and gaze all the way to the door. It was romantic, exciting, explosive and crazy. I loved every second of it.

One Wednesday morning, shortly before dawn, the inevitable happened. Hubby came home early to find his wife flat on her back on the living room floor in a half-discarded black lace negligee with me on top, pumping away at her open pussy with my brand new strap-on dildo. We bounded apart and jumped to our feet. I hurried into my jeans and t-shirt. She reached for a black and red chiffon robe flung over a chair and casually slipped into it. He shouted at her and called her names. She lit a cigarette, blew smoke in his face, and shouted back. He raised his arms above his head as he yelled. For a moment I thought he might hit her. Then I realized he was crying. He lowered his hands, covered his face, and stood in the middle of the room sobbing like a child. Cecile went over, put her arms around him, pulling him close, talking sweetly, telling him not to worry, everything was going to be all right.

I left quietly.

The next day, I swore off straight women forever.

J O A N N E S T L E

A Different Place

JAY LAY BACK IN THE TUB, the hot water soaking her tired muscles. It had been a long day on the job, a day that seemed to consist of moving a hundred two-by-fours made of steel. She smiled, proud of what her forty-year-old body could still do. She discovered more and more of its strengths every day. Already her forearms were solid and her back was hard and broad. She loved construction work, loved to see the houses change shape under the guidance of her hands, loved to solve a problem of angles first with her mind and then with her tools. But she was still glad when quitting time came, particularly today. Her girlfriend from New York was spending the night, was, in fact, waiting for her in the bedroom.

She spread her legs, letting the hot water push against her, watched it circle her breasts—all breasts and muscle, she grinned. Not a bad combination. She was going to use both of them tonight. She knew what her honey wanted and was more than willing to comply. In fact, she had a few new ideas. She let her head drop back against the tub's edge. Sometimes it was wonderful being butch, to know clearly what your women lovers had been saying to you over the years, to know what brought on the wetness and how to slip your hand under them so they began moving. Not that it was rote by now: every time was different, at least in the beginning.

"Would you like your back washed?"

She looked up in surprise. Carol stood in the doorway, dressed in a black slip, purple stockings, and lavender slingback heels. The slip with its thin straps cupped her breasts, the lace resting on their fullness. The half-hard nipples pushed against the silk, while the rest of the slip showed the fullness of the body underneath. Carol was a big woman, and at this moment her flesh was proud.

"No, that's okay, I'll be out in a minute."

They had only a short time together, and they both had already discovered that the best way of talking for them was making love. She laughed to herself. She knew a wanting femme when she saw one, but she also saw the love in Carol's eyes. Their love-making was not a test to see whether she could live up to her butch reputation. They knew months ago that they pleased each other that way. What she saw in Carol's eyes was desire, deep and stark, the sexual needing of an open woman. Carol wanted her, her hands, her arms, her breasts, her cunt, her tongue. This, Carol had made clear. She remembered the first time she had lifted Carol's legs back onto her chest, opening her up completely and then laying over her so she could feel Carol's wetness and the fullness of her clit under her. She did not need Carol to tell her that something special had happened that night, that cherishing and celebration had moved with them on that bed.

She slowly raised herself out of the tub, her tall body emerging from the heat. Sometimes life was hard, sometimes the loneliness and disappointments bore down on her like a lead sky, but tonight she felt good. She slowly dried herself and then sat on the closed toilet seat, taking long hauls on the joint she always treated herself to after a hard day. She knew Carol did not mind waiting, that expectation was a wonderful sharpener of desire. She ran her nails over her lips, checking for ragged edges. Then she carefully clipped any offending corners. She was taking responsibility for at least that part of the evening. Long ago she had learned that lovemaking was a combination of knowing the body's angles and curves and of pushing at its boundaries. Finally ready, she stood up, put a comb through her hair, and strolled into the bedroom. She paused in the doorway and just stood looking at the black-slipped woman who was lying on her stomach in the middle of the large bed. Her hips were moving slightly, and the slip had pulled up, exposing her full thighs above the purple stockings.

"How's my New York slut doing?" she said, in a low voice, as she circled the bed.

"Have you finished with all your preparations?" Carol answered, turning her head into the pillows. Then softly, "I want you."

"I know, baby, but I need just to watch you a little. I am going to sit in this chair and watch you grind your hips into that bed. I want to watch you move."

Dusk fell into the room. The only sounds were the rustling of the slip and Jay's breathing. Then Carol started making little moaning sounds. Soon the words, "Please, please don't make me wait any longer," were heard. Jay quickly got up and lowered herself onto Carol's back. Her long broad body completely covered the woman beneath her. She secured Carol's hands above her head with her own, and just using the strength of her body and mouth, she started to take the woman beneath her. She bit into Carol's neck and cheek. She thrust her tongue into Carol's ear. And all the time Carol never stopped moving below her. She rode with her, her own wetness seeping onto Carol's legs, onto the slip. She put her hand between Carol's legs, running her fingers from the woman's cunt to her more protected place of entry. She felt Carol's body strain under her, almost lifting them both up as she tried to give Jay more room for touching.

"Tonight I am going to fuck you in a different place," she whispered into Carol's ear, "but you have to want it." She brought her wet fingers back to Carol's asshole and pushed at its surface. Carol's body stiffened under her while at the same time Carol thrust herself back on Jay's finger.

"You tell me when you're ready. You let me know when you can take it." She kept rubbing the soft skin, slipping in just the tip of her finger. Carol first moved her hips away and then slowly brought them back as if to test the promise of this new intrusion. Jay's own wetness shone on Carol's ass and she swelled with the knowledge of the entry to come.

"Give me your ass to tell me you are ready," she said gently, her head above Carol's turned face. There was a pause, a silence in the room, and then the sound of a deep intake of breath as Carol slid her hips back onto Jay's hand. The sign had been given.

Jay positioned herself carefully over the woman's back, her arm drew back and the muscles that had lifted beams now poised for a more delicate power. She pushed her finger, blunt and strong, into Carol, feeling the tight resistance of the ass muscles, the strong sentinels protecting the soft world inside. Carol moaned, a different sound from when Jay penetrated her cunt. This was deeper, almost as if the body was finding a new voice for this more guarded entry.

"Yes, baby, here." She pushed harder. Carol was helping now by moving her ass back and forth, her whole back coming up under Jay's body, her arms stretching out above her head. Then Jay's finger was through—a wonderful mixture of tightness and tenderness grasped her. She moved in and out, penetrating a little more with each stroke. Carol's moans became louder. She tossed her head wildly, pushing the pillows up against the wall. Her whole body was pointed at Carol's finger, and now femme hunger was in control. Carol's full free body rocked under Jay, until suddenly, Carol raised herself up to her knees, forcing Jay back. Now it was clear that Carol wanted it all. She was thrusting her ass back and forth onto Jay's finger with her own rhythm, her breasts hanging full, dancing with each surge backward.

Jay looked down, watching and wondering at the strength of a woman's want. With her free hand she reached under Carol and opened her cunt lips. Wetness dripped down onto the sheets. Carol was rocking quietly now, all hips and ass, and joy flowed through Jay's fingers, her arms. She had brought this woman to her pleasure, and she was going to bring her home. Everything became quiet. Only the sound of movement could be heard, and then Jay felt all of Carol tighten around her finger. "Oh, God," the woman said, and fell forward, pulling Jay with her.

"Baby, so good, so good."

Slowly, carefully, Jay moved out, stopping to let Carol rest as her ass muscles first fought release and then let her go with all her power. She fell over Carol, and they both lay that way for many minutes. Carol at first was still moving as if a phantom finger was inside of her. Jay could feel her ass muscles clench and grow loose over and over again. She heard her own breathing come back to normal and became aware of the longing in her own body. She liked the sweat that trickled between them, the river of their desire, liked the feeling of her breasts and muscles on this woman who had made a home for her in her body. She liked the smell in the room. Someday she would offer her own ass, but for now, she rested and loved.

MARLYS LA BRASH

Friday's Fantasy

IT'S FRIDAY AND WITH ONE LAST LOOK around the office I head for the elevator, hit the button, and wait. The door opens, I step in, push "lobby," and settle in for the long solitary ride down. I look up as the door begins to close and who do I see but my boss, Ms. Wedgewood, moving with long, purposeful strides toward the elevator. I know I should hit the open button but I'm frozen. I can't move a muscle. Her long, slender, perfectly manicured hand slides between the almost closed doors. I gulp and finally snap out of it, reach up and push the button. The door opens, releasing her trapped hand. She steps in, and turns slightly. "Thank you, Carole," she says. "I'm glad not to be the only one left." I open my mouth to speak, only nothing comes out; my throat is like the Sahara desert, dry. All I can manage is a weak smile. I focus on the nape of her neck while I try to regain my composure.

I steal a sidelong glance in the mirror. My eyes take in the profile of her beautiful face and long silken neck visible above her collar. My heart skips a beat, my breath catches. The outline of her breasts can be seen pushing against the smooth fabric of her blouse. I can feel my face flush. My gaze drops to her slim waist and ample curve of her hips. Desire floods through me.

I take a deep, silent breath. It's now or never. With graceful ease, I drop my bag to the floor and with quiet resolve, take a step forward, closing the gap between us. We are inches apart. She senses my presence and stiffens slightly as my hot breath caresses her neck. I place my hands on her hips. All I can hear is the sound of our breathing echoing in the small space. I'm anticipating rejection, but instead she leans back. I place my hand on her thigh and, as I trace imaginary patterns, her entire body quivers with expectation.

I reach up, lightly grip her upper arms, and meeting no resistance, slowly, gently, I turn her to face me. I'm stunned at the intensity of her light grey-blue eyes. I pull myself from her riveting stare, her long, thick lashes brushing across high cheek bones, her full sensual lips enticing me on.

I hesitate for just a moment before I continue my journey. Her eyes are half-closed, head tilted to one side, cheeks aglow, tip of her tongue resting on her upper lip. There is no protest as I unbutton her blouse, my hands trembling as I open her bra. I ease the lacy cups aside, releasing her breasts. Taking one in my hand, I tenderly massage her soft flesh. Leaning down, I take the other breast in my mouth, my lips teasing an already swollen nipple hard. A gasp escapes her lips and with each caress of my tongue she shivers. I withdraw my hand and move downward, tracing a sensuous path, coming to rest at the swell of her hip. Reluctantly my lips leave her breast to explore, my mouth hungry for the sweet taste of her skin. Tauntingly, I nibble. Tremors race across her stomach. She moans with pleasure. It's the only sound I hear in the electrified air.

I drop to my knees, no longer able to stand, and slide one hand under her skirt, the other grasping the zipper, opening it, tooth by tooth . . . *ping*. . . . "LOBBY," states the disembodied voice. I groan as the doors open. I'm desperately trying to maintain some fragile control. Ms. Wedgewood steps out into the sun-filled lobby. She turns. Her face is flushed and a thin layer of sweat covers her upper lip.

"Have a good weekend, Carole. . . . Oh, and thanks for letting me share."

Awkwardly, I clear my throat. My voice husky, I wish her the same. Just for a moment I feel as if she knew. No, couldn't be.

BONNIE WATERSTONE

I Have a Crush on You

I CAN'T BELIEVE YOU'RE GOING TO QUIT, that we won't work side by side, the slope of your hips so near. As you leave, I want to tell you everything. How I've been in love with you for three years. The dream that started it all—how I woke up feeling joined with you, as if you knew me clear through—and all we were doing was walking down a hallway to a door outside, our steps in rhythm, talking intently. The door opened, I opened. And then my nightly ritual, engraving your name with my fingers between my legs. How I have called to you. Don't leave, I want to say. I have a crush on you.

I want to stroke your naked body, the skin I've never seen, I want to slide my hands down those broad, bulky hips. I want to know the colour and texture of your cunt hair, to feel its tickle on my nose. I want to tease you until your sentences became less than complete, until your careful British cadences break into syllables that are not so precise. I want to hear you cry out words that don't make sense, as you pull me down, push my head between your legs, squeeze the breath out of me with your strong thighs.

But you are taken. Your long-term commitment to Marlene is legendary. Lesbians in this small, rural community whisper the story in awe: seventeen years; moved to the country together, bought land;

built your own house, plumbing, electricity, and all; cultivate a perfect garden. I imagine a threesome, myself as the younger partner, maybe apprentice, joining you and Marlene, helping out around the place. I could be next to you even on the days when we're not working together in the library. I would do anything to be near you.

At work, the closer I dared stand to you the more charge I felt. You must have felt the heat, as my heart spelled out your name in double time. I know we were talking about work, but I'd talk to you about anything. Your clipped tones and complete sentences charmed me, that little laugh in your eyes waiting to break into a smile. I would plot little "touch events," orchestrating a moment when my hand would brush yours as I reached for something. Just thinking about that left me wet and waiting for you, for the turn of your head and the smile into my eyes. Sometimes in the frenzied hectic rushing around to serve the last library users before closing we'd bump hips; I'd feel your bones beneath the firm padding of your flesh. "Sorry," you'd apologize briskly, focused on your work. I'd forget the task at hand, smile secretly, savouring that brief contact, lost again in those hips I loved to watch. Or in meetings, contemplating your bent head as you wrote minutes, the way your hair changed to grey as it curved around your ears: your ear, what it might be like to trace that ear with my tongue, to be near that pulse in your neck, to feel it with my lips.

How will I live without your weathered hand against the flat whiteness of a piece of paper as you talk to me about a project and I fall into the web between your fingers, nestle next to your knuckles, catch my breath as you stop speaking and look at me: "I'm sorry, I didn't hear what you said. . . ." You smile indulgently. Did you/do you know?

ROSALYN SANDRA LEE

A Hidden Kiss

SHE STOOD CLOSE, TOO CLOSE for a first date. The heat was getting to me and it wasn't just the warmth of that summer night. Thank goodness I was leaning on the car or I'm sure I would have fallen. From what I couldn't be sure of at that time. From the weather surrounding me or the temperature rising inside of me? Was I flush from fever or had it been that long since a woman had touched me that way? The tingle between my legs answered any questions and squelched all doubt about my swinging head. The scent of her circled my soul. My long-held passions were about to surrender, willingly.

My hands dropped to my sides and instinct took over as I cupped her hips with the palms of my hands. I watched my hands take on a life of their own, as my fingers performed their own "Nutcracker Suite," dancing and twirling with light, swift, purposeful movement, as they traced her body. I wrapped her in my arms, breathing heavily on the back of her neck. My heart skipped a beat while my legs fought to support my now jelly-like body, when she turned and brushed my nipples ever so lightly with sure intentions. We were so excited, I'm surprised my rock hard nipples didn't jump from their harness like untamed horses, but I was as cool as I could possibly pretend to be.

Earlier that day, we met for lunch and all she did was stare at me across the table. I was flattered but could not eat for the stares. I finally asked why she was staring and she said I was cute. After lunch, we walked to the seaport, where I got so caught up in her look, I almost kissed her right there. Until one of my co-workers walked up on us. That jolted me. Or was it her knees rubbing my thigh that brought me back to earth? I knew it wouldn't be long before our lips were introduced with intent to getting to know the other's, intimately.

Our eyes locked and I could feel the pull, much like planets have on objects that get within range. Noticing the target, waiting patiently, then locking on with an invisible tractor beam. "Lord help me, I'm being sucked in." My lips moved in closer. I was so close I could almost hear her heart beat, but I'm sure it was my own, pounding in anticipation.

Were those fireworks? Or an explosion of passion? Our lips became magnets. As we stood holding hands, our faces glued together by the soft sweetness our tongues had to offer. We danced inside slowly, but with purpose. I felt her exploring every cavern of my mouth, turning my tongue with her own, nibbling my lip then coming back inside for more. If we were to have broken any laws that morning in the streets of the Big Apple, I knew it would be worth the night in jail.

Soon I felt her lips on my cheeks, offering warm delight to my eyelids, my nose, under my chin and back to my lips. Her tongue just seemed to swell so large. Suddenly those heavenly kisses turned into big licks of . . . *dog!* I jumped up from my sleep to find my chocolate Lab licking my face, nudging me with his nose and his leash on the bed.

"Morning already? Damn, I love you dearly, but you sure know how to ruin a woman's day." I trudged off to answer Mother Nature's call, to find my day hadn't been ruined at all.

MERRIL MUSHROOM

The Saleslady

THE SALESLADY WAS BEAUTIFUL. She was helping me look through winter coats on the reduced rack toward the rear of the store when it happened:

I was pulling a green and brown down-filled number toward me when it slipped from the hanger. The saleslady and I both reached for it at the same time, and at that moment, my hand accidentally grazed the side of her breast. An immediate jolt of heat, unexpected, coursed up my arm, and I felt the sudden hardness of her nipple as she turned. She gasped, and my hand moved with a life of its own to cup her breast. I was acutely aware of her soft flesh beneath the fabric of blouse and brassiere, taut tip straining against the material and radiating a warmth which seemed like liquid against the creases of my palm.

Continuing to turn, the saleslady brushed my face with her breath, stopped, and caught my mouth suddenly with her own. Her lips were hot, demanding, eager. Then both of us were pulling apart from each other, drawing in long, quivering breaths as we separated. "Why don't you meet me in the dressing room, baby," I murmured.

She took a crimson suede jacket from its hanger and pressed it against my chest. "Take this into number five," she said softly. "I'll be right there."

Number five was a short distance away from the rest of the booths. I opened it and entered. There was a full-length mirror along the back wall of the tiny space and a short bench set against the side wall. I hung the jacket over the hook on the back of the door, and almost immediately the door opened and the saleslady slipped inside. She leaned against the door and looked me over, then smiled and stepped toward me. Her arms wrapped around my neck, her body pressed against my length, and her face nuzzled between my neck and shoulder.

My arms went around her, pulled her close. She moaned a soft, little sound. With tiny, moist kisses, she brought her lips up my neck, around my ear, over my cheek, and against my lips. She opened her mouth wide, and I felt her breath hot in the back of my throat. She clawed her hands up through my hair, long fingernails pressing against my scalp, and I dug my fingertips into her flesh. She began to tremble, and I shifted to brace us against the wall.

I pulled away from her then, looked at her face. She laughed softly, touched my mouth, my cheek, my throat with red-tipped talons, then suddenly raked her nails down my chest and over my breast. I caught her wrist, turned her hand away, and bent over her, trapping her arm behind her back. She grabbed the front of my shirt with her other hand and pulled, forcing my head forward, and again mashed her mouth against mine.

Again I moved away. She bleated deep in her throat, moaned loudly. "Shhh!" I pulled her face to my shoulder, and she took shirt and flesh between her teeth. "Don't make a sound," I whispered in her ear, "or they'll hear you in the store." I plunged my tongue into her ear then, and she gripped my hair with trembling fingers, then clutched her palm over my shoulder and down my arm to guide my hand to her belt. She squeezed my wrist urgently.

Quickly I unfastened her belt, the snap of her pants, eased the zipper down. I drew my fingertips over her quivering skin, reached beneath the elastic band of her panties, moved slowly down until my fingers found the top of her pubic hair. I held my hand still then, and rested my palms and fingers against the heat of her belly. She gasped, pressing hard against me. I leaned back slightly, so I could slip my hand between her thighs, feeling the slick, damp fabric of her panties against the back of my fingers, feeling her moisture fill my palm.

"Shhh," I reminded her, "don't make a sound." I kissed her again, pushing my tongue into her mouth as I slid my fingers through the wetness of her cunt, stroked her, stroked her and entered her, stifling her cries with my lips. Then I moved again, pinning her with my gaze. "You must be absolutely silent," I commanded the saleslady, "or they'll hear you in the store." With my fingers still inside her, I used my other hand to pull her jeans and underpants down over her hips and buttocks and, in one smooth, butch movement, raised my leg to stand onto the crotch of her pants, pulling them down her thighs and to her feet.

"Sssss!" Her breath hissed sharply through her teeth as she fought to control the sounds rising from her throat. I covered her mouth with my own again, bent her back against the wall, and pushed my knees between her thighs, parting her legs as much as possible against the jeans and panties constraining her ankles. She rose to me with all her strength then, and I took her hard and fast, while she tore at my hair and the back of my shirt, filled her mouth with the flesh of my neck and shoulder to muffle her cries; until she came in a burst against my palm, and I stroked her softly until she came again and still again. She caught my wrist then, and pulled my hand away, laid the side of her face against my shoulder, and sighed. After a moment, she kissed me tenderly on the mouth, reached down, and pulled up her clothing. Fastening her pants and belt, she pushed the door open and slipped out.

I pulled out my pocket comb and ran it through my hair, savouring her aroma on my fingers. When I left the store a few minutes later, without a winter coat but with a sweet, warm feeling inside me, the saleslady was up front with another customer. As I passed by, she winked at me. I winked back.

S U S A N L E E

Restaurant Rendezvous

I WAS IN A RESTAURANT having coffee with some friends when I noticed her sitting at the bar. She kept looking in my direction, so I glanced over my shoulder to see what she was gazing at. Surprisingly, she was staring at me. She was incredibly gorgeous and while I sat there peering into my coffee wondering what to do next, I noticed she was gone. I quickly scanned the restaurant to see where she was and saw her standing in a doorway leading down a flight of stairs. She smiled and started down, so I got up and followed.

By the time I reached the bottom she was nowhere in sight. I looked around and saw a door that was slightly opened. I walked over and took a couple of tentative steps in when suddenly the door shut behind me. I knew it was her when I heard the "click" of the lock.

I stood wondering what was next, as my heart raced in anticipation. I thought she could hear it, the fast beating—thump, thump, thump. I could feel her breathing gentle puffs of air that tickled the back of my neck. The sweet smell of her perfume pulled me and I leaned into her, with my head tilted, waiting for her kiss. Her lips softly, slowly, moved from my ear to my shoulder and granted me the soft wet kiss I was waiting for.

I let out a little moan as she ran her hands along my shoulders and arms. Her fingers left tingling trails down to the back of my hands. She felt so good with her arms wrapped around me. I turned in her arms and kissed her rich, full mouth. An electric shock ran through my stomach. We were both breathing heavy and hard.

Her hands caressed my back, waist, and hips while her lips and tongue rolled with mine. Her fingers found the buttons on my shirt and unfastened them one by one, while her lips brushed my chest and her tongue teased my nipples. She traced her hands across my stomach, along the waistband of my jeans. I didn't move as they dropped to the floor.

She slid to the throbbing she'd created between my legs, and I shuddered as she slipped her hand between my thighs, softly stroking and teasing me. I felt myself being carried away by the rhythm she was creating. Rocking back and forth, I pushed down as she moved a little faster. I let out a groan. She was driving me crazy. I was on the edge. She moved her hand away, smiled mischievously, and kissed my pouting mouth.

She pressed her leg between my wet thighs and I rubbed against her, so close yet so far. She took her leg away and quickly replaced it with her tongue, which slowly circled my clit. I was slipping away into that final moment of ecstasy when she stopped for a second to slide in one finger, then two, working me until I cried out in delirious pleasure.

My knees buckled, and she managed to catch me before I fell to the floor. We held onto each other for a while, giggling, and then kissed goodbye. She left the room while I gathered myself together and I wasn't too surprised to find her gone when I got upstairs. So I happily rejoined my friends with a grin on my face, ready with a new topic of conversation.

JESS WELLS

The Agent

THERE ISN'T A NEW YORKER ALIVE who would fault me for it, and San Franciscans might cut me some slack as well, but I have actually fucked for real estate.

I couldn't help it.

It wasn't just desperation in the face of a small down payment, high expectations, a town with water on at least three sides and a no-growth urban policy. It was that the process was so sexual.

Why do real estate agents have cars with interiors of better leather than my sex toys? I was being transported in a high-class dildo bag—*I Dream of Jeannie*'s bottle if Jeannie were a dominatrix. She kept saying I would have to open myself to the possibility of love, and I tried to remember that she was talking about loving a house. "Imagine yourself there," she said, handing me coffee, turning on my music, pampering me like I imagine Hollywood babes get treated. She drove me around town, then led me into the houses. "Can you see your bed here?" she'd say, sweeping a long muscular arm around a sunny room, and there was something clandestine about it right away. These were other people's homes. Their owners were at work. And we were in their bedroom in the midddle of the day. Or they were vacant homes with polished floors and she would pop her little butt up onto the kitchen counter and cross her long legs, shake her foot, and describe dinner parties I might have. "A quarter million," she'd say, "and I can get you financing, easy."

Well, I'm sorry but all that money is so sexy. Makes you feel powerful, legitimate. Capable. It goes into your pants, it does. Besides, nothing about my financing is easy, so when she said that, it was as if she were giving me a quarter mill, not just a house; she was giving the dinner party, the bedroom, she was my wife providing the sunny Sunday mornings she described as she took me through the houses.

"Are you open?" she kept asking. Open to the possibilities?

She wore perfume, or the smell of leather hung on her, maybe she put weed in the car's air supply or something because I wanted her. Right there in a stranger's kitchen, on some old lady's dining table, in an empty room where this beautiful bed in my suddenly beautiful life would hold her sleek nakedness. I was being led around town, through moist basements and narrow secret hallways, by my nose like an idiot bull, and I fucked her during "agent appointments" on seven butcher blocks and three wood floors, in a "bonus room down" and in one dilapidated shed before I got the fever and really wanted her bad.

I wanted her like I wanted a solid foundation, a quick escrow with buckets of cash back from the seller for nothing. I wanted to wheel and deal her on the end of my tongue.

Then she found the place for me. She fucked me so hard in this darling old house that some biddy had died in, just nailed me so good that I laid there on that old area rug, lookin' at heaven through little French doors. Might not have been the doors, but it was French something, so I signed on the dotted line. Moved in like a mistress being settled somewhere.

She was good to me.

Visited me after broker's opens on Tuesdays.

Then I started to follow her. I thought I would surprise her, play a little cat and mouse during an inspection or something, see if I couldn't lay her out in the gazebo. I saw her pull her motored sex toy in front of a house. A sign in front said SOLD. I missed my parking spot and had to circle the block but as I passed the house, I saw the door open, saw some woman's hand cup the agent's head and pull her into the house.

Very intimate gesture, this cupping of heads.

My agent was in there for nearly an hour, then dashed for her car, pulling out her cell phone. The woman tripped out of the house all dolled up—pert and pressed—made me want to puke. Got in the sex toy and they toured. I was speechless. I followed her. My agent, a lock box, into a house and then out again with the client all glassy-eyed, reaching for the agent's hand, but my agent dodged a bit when they parted. Then my girl's off to another house where she takes down a SOLD sign. Then some ho comes out, flings her arms around my gal in real estate.

That's all I need to see.

I stopped by the stationary store on the way home. I believe escrow has closed, I whined to myself. Two boxes of Kleenex, big bottle of Visine, and a FOR SALE BY OWNER sign for the front of my house.

Homo-ownership, my ass.

A U G U S T   N O I R

Sex Club

We are in an anonymous but far from neutral place: a sex club. Yes. You've gone cruising, unaware of my presence, or rather honouring our thief's pact—you have agreed to pretend that I am not here, too. You wander and look, your body tense, though only I really sense it. You appear casual, relaxed, bemused. I hover and track you as you glide through the darkened rooms, occasionally stopping to watch the frantic, intent couplings. I watch you from corners, hidden in shadow. I obscure myself in order to maintain an illusion—a good one, solid and monumental—of anonymity, detachment, cool disinterest. I am just another blasé voyeur. But for the tense specificity, the surgical precision in the focus of my gaze, I could be anyone, any stranger, watching you watch random sexual encounters in which you are not yet a participant. You will be, soon. I recognize the potential in the strange glitter in your eyes, the twitching half-smile that plays across your mouth. You are hungry, curious, intrigued, controlled. I am just as hungry, even more controlled.

At last someone approaches you. A tough-looking butch with a buzzcut gets in your path and refuses to move, fixing you in place with the force of her carnal imperative. I can't see her face clearly, and truthfully, it doesn't matter what she looks like, it doesn't much matter what she says to you. She is incidental to my possession of you, so she remains shadowy. But now the image of your face becomes unnaturally clear to me, the shifting sensations that animate its loveliness: surprise, anger, lust, fear, pleasure deepened by hot waves of guilt and shame. You are going to get yourself fucked, very publicly. She pushes you up against a wall, slings your leg roughly over her muscular thigh. A faceless butch—my anonymous agent, my stand-in.

With the full force of her lust, she pins your firm, small body, that envelope of flesh I know so well, to the wall. She yanks up your skirt roughly. Of course, you've worn nothing else underneath: you're nothing if not calculating. Even from where I watch several feet away, I can see how you shift your hips slightly to make yourself more available to her, how ready and wet you are. She enters you abruptly, with none of the gentleness, no tender kiss or sweet sigh or soft murmur, no breath-whispered "yes" which you require me to extract. No working you up with two or three fingers; the gloved fist grinds into you imperiously, raw and not a little rough. You are complicit, willing. You want to be violated. One arm locked firmly against the small of your back, she pumps. Leisurely at first, then more insistently, more urgently. You are enjoying it, despite yourself, despite the pain and your thinly-veiled internal discomfort rising with the revelation: you crave a sexual free-fall without the safety net of love, raw desire without the comforting cloak of tenderness.

I stand in mute witness. I can see your face clearly from my vantage point, intermittently concealed by passing bodies. People are collecting; the two of you have become the spectacle of the moment. I remain utterly still, do not move, barely breathe. I implode at the sight of your acquiescence, your not altogether passive receipt of another's desire and capacity to penetrate your conceit of independence. Her motions are insistent, the staccato cadence of pure lust. Your body absorbs their violent rhythms. Head thrown back, neck tensed, back arched, your arms are down, palms flat against the wall. Your blonde hair teased against the rough surface with each quickening thrust. Your gaze seems vaguely focused on something above the swelling ranks of voyeurs, but your eyes register nothing.

Then you start to come. I know that gritty determined look and the exquisite tension of your silence. Just as you begin to let go, at the exact instant when your consciousness dissolves and you get lost in sharp pleasure, I move into your sightline. I want you to see me, to return my gaze. I want you to acknowledge that I am the one fucking you, through the apparition of my desire. We lock eyes: hold the gaze as fiercely as an animal grips its kill, bloody rent flesh, in clamped jaws.

The stud slowly pulls her hand out. Your body slumps slightly, a slow-leaking balloon. A smattering of appreciative sighs from the gallery. Show's over. But before you can re-establish yourself, before you emerge completely from the reverie of release, before you regain the precious illusion of control, you close your eyes for one brief instant. When you open them I am gone, disappearing with the image of your exposure. I steal away with your nakedness, your need, your desire, your shame and guilt, your travail of illicit pleasure. I smuggle it out, burned into my retinas. I possess it. You will have to reach deep inside me to retrieve it.

I'll be waiting for you at home.

KITTY TSUI

The Cutting

WHEN BROOKE FIRST CAME OUT into the scene almost a decade ago, there were many things she thought were plain revolting: piercing—temporary and permanent—branding, canes, water sports, scat, and cutting.

She had a friend who very much enjoyed being cut. Her friend sported the scars proudly all over her body. One day she held a cutting party. Brooke politely declined. But when the night came Brooke was alone. Her date for the evening had canceled, so she went to the party for food, drink, and the company.

When it was time for the cutting to begin, Brooke positioned herself in the front row, much to her surprise. As the scalpel cut into the woman's flesh and blood seeped from the thin lines drawn on her skin, Brooke's eyes never left her back. Throughout the two-hour-long process, Brooke was spellbound. And from that moment on, she was hooked.

Beginning a couple of years after that, Brooke actively searched for someone to do a cutting on her. But somehow it had never worked out. Until she met Adrian.

It was Adrian's forty-second birthday and a party had been thrown in her honour. Brooke went with a mutual friend. When Adrian and

Brooke were introduced, a current shot through Brooke's body. They held on to each other's hand for what seemed like a long time. When Adrian walked away to greet her other guests, Brooke watched her. She wore a white shirt, black pants, and boots. Her bearing was erect, her stride sure.

Brooke watched her all night long. The silver in her dark hair caught the light. She moved with an easy confidence, and her laughter carried across the room, brushing Brooke's ears like silk.

The next evening they went to dinner at a Chinese restaurant. After they had finished eating and were opening their fortune cookies, Brooke asked: "So, Adrian, Susan told me you were interested in playing? Is that correct?"

That's something Brooke loved about leather-women. They put it right out there. No dicking around or beating around the bush. *Want to play? Yes. When? How about now? Sure. Want to fuck? Yes. Got gloves and lube? Great.* Vanilla girls could learn a few things.

"Yes," she replied without hesitation. "I am."

So they did.

On the first date they did a flogging scene. The next night Brooke got a combo. Adrian gave her a great massage and one of the best fucks she'd ever experienced. The night after that, Adrian did a cutting on her.

"You're an experienced player, and very popular it seems. Why choose me to do it?" Adrian asked.

"I've wanted it for a long time," Brooke responded, "but I've never met the right person. I feel connected to you. I want to know what it feels like. I want it to be with you but I can't explain why."

"Why do you want a cutting?" Adrian continued.

"I have a fascination with sharp edges. Swords, switchblades, straight razors. I've played with knives, but not when they've broken the skin. I want to experience it. I want to know what the sensation's like. And I love the taste of blood. You don't know how much I loved eating out a woman who was bleeding."

"Umm, yes, I miss that too. In fact I miss going down on a woman, period. I can do without the experience of dental dams."

"Yeah. I haven't eaten pussy in years. I hate latex, so I just don't do it at all."

"More's the pity." Adrian touched her arm. "Well, my dear, here's your chance to taste blood again. There's nothing safer than your own."

She lay Brooke down on the bed and kissed her. Adrian's tongue moved into her mouth and she sucked, savored it as if it were treacle.

"Just remember to keep breathing," she whispered. "I'm right here with you."

Adrian covered both her hands with latex gloves. When she removed the scalpel from its wrapping, Brooke held her breath. Adrian brought the light closer, leaned over, and smiled.

"Adrian, I'm scared," Brooke said.

"Yes, and so you should be. A blade is a dangerous thing."

The edge of it touched Brooke's skin. It felt like a pointed pencil until Adrian pressed down and Brooke drew in a sharp breath. The experience was neither a burning sensation nor an icy pain. There was an intensity to the sensation that defied description.

Adrian drew the Chinese character for love on Brooke's left breast. In blood. Four strokes that she recut four times. Then she brought out a switchblade, scraped up the blood, and placed the edge of it on Brooke's tongue. The blood tasted metallic. She wanted more.

"Make me bleed again. Please," Brooke begged.

"I think that's enough for your first time," Adrian said firmly, a smile playing on her lips. "If I didn't know you were a top, I'd accuse you of being a greedy bottom."

"Right now that's exactly how I feel."

"Good. I hope you feel like a masochist too because I'm about to pour alcohol on it."

The coldness of the rubbing alcohol combined with the stinging heat when it hit Brooke's flesh gave her a jolt. It was definitely a combination of pain and pleasure.

"Will it scar?"

"Probably not this time. But if I recut it after it's healed it might."

"I want the mark of it to be permanent. It's my first and I want to keep it. I want to keep something from you," Brooke added shyly.

"I could rub salt on it."

"Salt! Are you kidding?"

"No, I take my play very seriously, but I'd have to tie you down first."

Salt! And the woman's not kidding? What am I doing in her bed? a voice in Brooke's head screamed. *Get out of here. Get out right away.*

"Ah, I see that scared you, didn't it? The thought of me rubbing salt into your open cuts. Why don't you just anticipate that then. I'll do you when you heal. I'll recut you and then rub salt into your skin. Frightening, isn't it? But I bet you're wet just thinking about it. Aren't you?"

Brooke nodded her head. She had been wet for some time, gloriously wet.

Adrian put down the scalpel. Her latex-clad hand travelled down Brooke's body. She found her wetness and plunged inside. Then pulled out and went in search of her clit.

"Are you breathing?" she asked. "Oh, you're swollen and so hard."

"Adrian, Adrian," Brooke moaned, "if you keep touching me there I'm going to come."

"Not without asking you're not."

"Oh, I can't, I can't hold on much longer."

"Then ask. Say my name and ask for permission."

"Adrian. . . ."

"Yes?"

"I . . . I'm going to come. Oh, Adrian, can I? Can I?"

She rubbed Brooke harder, faster. "Yes, yes. Come for me now." As the contractions gripped her, Brooke called out her name. "AdrianAdrianAdrianAdrianAdrian."

Later that week, Brooke made a journal entry:

"I'm back at home now. Adrian and I live in different cities. But I bear the mark of her still.

"Love, on my breast."

M. ANNE VESPRY

Apple for Teacher

THE CLOCK TICKS TOWARD SIX; I'm still at school. Listening to the janitor clattering away to the first floor. Watching dust motes weave in the evening light. Wondering why Ms. Watson has nothing better to do than keep me in detention.

The sway of her breasts catches my attention as she reaches for another book. All she needs to do is come to the bar and every dyke in town will be asking her out. Even here, half the punks have crushes on her. Emphasizing my thoughts, a worshipper's apple gleams on her desk.

"Corey! Are you finished? I have work for you if you have nothing better to do than dream."

Shit. Caught staring. "No, Ms. Watson." No, I haven't finished—and no, I haven't anything better to do than dream about your body.

Funny how my insolent tone flusters her. Maybe she knows more than she's letting on about why I'm here. After all, they find guns and junk in lockers every day. What's so bad about my toys? Four hours of detention every evening for a month is serious.

If she does know, perhaps it's more than coincidence she took the job of monitoring me. It's strange she wanted the "evidence of my crime" in the room. Maybe she wants a demonstration. Maybe she's just waiting for me to make the first move. Maybe. . . . Fuck this dreaming, what can I lose?

My chair scrapes as I stand. At her angry glance, I mutter something about having to . . . and walk toward the door. She looks down again to her papers, then glances up in surprise when she hears the lock catch. I turn toward her, smiling, as I tuck the key into the pocket of my leather pants.

"What are you doing?" she asks as I swagger toward her. Her detention-monitor snarl quavers on the last word.

"I just thought," I say, resting one hip against her desk and picking up the apple, "that we might have more fun . . . talking." I take a bite of the apple and savour it. Chewing slowly, I take an obvious inventory of her body. She stares, absorbed in the contrast between my black leather glove and her polished red apple. Something in the situation must have aroused her. By the time my gaze returns to her breasts, her nipples are erect and visible through her thin cotton blouse.

"You're not here to talk, sit down and . . . "

Whatever she was going to say is choked off as I stick the apple in her mouth. "Keep it in," I tell her, "or I'll find something worse." I stand, grab her nipples, and slowly guide her upright. "We both know you want me to fuck you silly. Right?" She nods, amazing me and, from the look on her face, amazing herself.

"Good, 'cause I'm about to do it."

I grab her collar and rip her blouse open. Stepping behind her, I yank the ruined shirt down, using it to bind her arms together. Undoing her skirt takes only a moment longer. As it settles around her ankles, I push her forward across the desk.

Trusting the weight of her anticipation to hold her, I pick up my toy bag and spread its contents across the desk. Leather cuffs buckle securely onto her ankles and wrists. Thank the gods, there's enough rope to attach the cuffs to the legs of her desk. Nothing like playing in a new (and unplanned) room to bring out a top's anxieties. Wanting to watch her expression, I flip her while tying her down. Now she watches me, arousal and fear alternating in her eyes, as I pull my belt knife and surgical gloves out of the bag. Her fear builds as I unsheathe the knife and drag its dull side teasingly down her chest and across her stomach. The cold steel raises goose bumps on her skin, then cuts neatly through her practical white cotton underwear. I pull them off, and sheath the knife.

I lean over her, warming her with my body, letting her rub herself on my leathers. I stroke her, enjoying the feel of her skin through my tight, calf-skin gloves; enjoying the sighing, moaning noises that come from behind the apple as I alternate between gentle caressing and hard, rough, twisting; most of all enjoying the idea of fucking my grade twelve English teacher.

Her ass is making wet, slapping noises on the desktop as she moves, trying to rub her dripping cunt against my body. I take off one leather glove, and pull on a latex one. The snap it makes startles her into biting through the apple. "Bad girl," I growl, stuffing my discarded leather glove in her mouth. "Bite on this." It looks good, and I'm not worried about any noise she might make past it. The janitor is far away, and I'm sure no one else is in the building.

I make a fist and rotate my hand above her face. I run my knuckles up and down her cunt, nudging her clit with each stroke, lubricating the latex with her wetness. Half a second pause, and I slide three fingers into her. We both moan. No matter how often I do this, I never get tired of the smooth hug of a woman's cunt around my fingers. Another finger, then my thumb, and her body sucks my hand in deeper. I hold for a moment, watching the amazement on her face change to a hunger I'd only dreamed of seeing. Her hips move and I let her set a pace for my thrusts. Her contractions grow stronger until I worry about broken bones as she comes. Gradually she relaxes and I slide my hand out.

"If you promise to be a good teacher I'll let you go now," I say, removing the leather from her mouth.

"What if I won't?"

Her defiance challenges me—adding determination to my reply. "You'd better like sucking cunt, getting whipped, and being fucked."

She smiles. "I think," she says, "We'll be having detentions for a long, long time."

FIONA LAWRY

Anglo Girl

I NOTICE THE PRETTY ANGLO GIRL on the peak hour train. She is absently regarding the Met Map beside her on the carriage wall—allowing me to look long at her. She is beautiful. I am fascinated by her. She is younger than me, well-dressed, executive, longish blonde hair, blue eyes.

I follow the line of her neck downward to the undulation of her breasts contained beneath her corporate jacket. Her skin is smooth, her jawline clean and strong. Long hands and long legs under her skirt. There's a slit up the centre of it, just like the one I'm imagining between her legs.

I move toward her in the crowded carriage and approach as if to take the seat next to her, instead stopping in the space directly in front. I pause for a moment and drink in the sensation of her warmth, her femininity. From my vantage point above her, I can see down her open-necked blouse. Her breasts sit cupped and pushed together in her blue lace bra.

At last feeling my gaze upon her, she breaks her stare and meets my eyes. I reach down and lightly brush her hair back off her shoulders before easing the corporate jacket apart. She flinches a little and flashes her blue eyes at me. Boldly, I continue. She is sitting quite still and upright. My hands move down and lightly brush over the form of her breasts beneath the smooth silkiness of her blouse. Her nipples push against the fabric like hard little buttons. I am faintly aware that her breathing has become harder and that her perfume has been infused with a warm muskiness.

A businessman in a dark blue suit crushes up against me in the crowding train and she parts her legs to make more room for me. We are both panting heavily and I can't believe that the other commuters seem not to see us at all. I like the close feeling of the big businessman's back pressed up against mine as I stand over her. I glance up and notice the train is passing through North Melbourne station. I haven't got much time.

I kneel down tight in front of her and feel my own cunt begin to throb and pulsate, as I slip my hands into her bra, cupping her breasts in the palms of my hands, feeling the fullness and weight of her. Her nipples harden as I rub and pinch. She gasps loudly and I smother the sound by covering her mouth with my own, plunging my tongue deep inside her.

She grips my body and pulls me to her with the strength of her legs. I bury my tongue in her warm wet cunt and hear the moaning and straining of the train pulling up at my station. Looking over at the seat beside the Met map, I realize that the girl must have got out at her stop while I was absorbed in my fantasy. I stand and dash off the carriage, just as the doors slam shut.

NISA DONNELLY

A Question of Balance

THE SUBWAY CAR, EMPTY when she first boarded, is filling with morning commuters. Huddled into her seat by the door, Francesca McClain is trying to disappear.

Her eyes toy with the lines in the book on her lap, Octavio Paz's *Sor Juana*. In the margin, next to a long and, to her mind, dull description of an ancient religious caste system and how it justifies his premise that the poet nun was somehow more chaste than Francesca imagines. She has written in her almost painfully neat script: "But why?" Marlene, when what she thought still mattered, used to chastise Francesca for writing in the margins of books, cramped script spilling down with unfinished thoughts, half-decipherable encoded messages. A terrible habit, she thinks, one picked up when she was still a student at the same university where she now guides petulant freshmen through a world of literature that they're too young to appreciate, certainly too young to understand. Or perhaps they are like this critic, blind to the obvious. Francesca's fingers pause over the poet's words to her beloved Vicereine: *This afternoon, you saw and touched my heart, dissolved and liquid in your hands.* Jerking to a stop, the subway sighs and moans as another dozen passengers press on board. Too crowded now to read, Francesca sighs and closes the book, the words "liquid in your hands" playing across her lips like a warm breath. It has been a long, very long time, since any woman has dissolved her heart, become liquid in her hands.

A woman in very high heels and a white crocheted dress balances herself next to Francesca's left shoulder. Delicate hands with long fingers and very red nail polish clutch the overhead bar. Full hips sway, keeping time with the train as it mambos through the darkened tunnel. The dress, loose, but not quite modest, stretches more than its owner probably imagines over naked flesh. Francesca smiles at the woman's secret, at the flash of skin and the deep shadows where her legs end, at the promise of what the lace could reveal. The bronzed woman leans low across Francesca to pull the stop cord, showing a flash of bare breast where the dress separates. Her skin would taste of salt and bitters, warm and slick, liquid in Francesca's hands. Black eyes fringed in black lashes look down, flutter, look away, then back, not quite nervous. The woman smiles, slow and easy.

"Trust me," the eyes whisper, and she opens her legs, straddling Francesca's naked thigh, stroking soft flesh, kneading dampening curls. Breasts, brown as toast, nipples puckered and pink, graze Francesca's back, until she trembles. A low, almost painful throb which Francesca thought she had lost or thrown away or hidden deeply, grows in her belly. How long since she's wanted a woman this way? How long since her skin has prickled and flushed? How long since she has dissolved liquid in any woman's hands? Too long.

Francesca closes her eyes and rocks into the woman, who tastes of salt and sin, who has magic hands. Too little magic left in the world. They're good together. Too good, almost, for strangers. Only the flesh, not the face, is familiar, and Francesca doesn't care. This woman wants her the way no woman has in too long. This is the woman who will bring Francesca McClain to her knees, who will push Marlene once, finally and certainly into the unforgiving past. Warm and sweet against bare flesh, Francesca buries her face in the woman's damp neck as the train jerks to a stop.

The woman whispers something Francesca can't quite hear. Smiling, she opens her eyes: "I'm sorry. What did you say?"

The bronzed woman is not smiling. "I asked if this is the Civic Center stop."

Francesca nods and pulls closer to the wall, as the woman evaporates out the door. She strains to see if the dress will part again, show one last flash of breast, a shadow of thigh. It doesn't. The subway jerks back to life. A fat man, smelling of sweat and garlic and Old Spice, crowds into the space vacated by the woman in the crocheted dress. Francesca opens the book again, feigning sudden fascination with the lines of text that swim before her. She dabs at her eyes. Foolish. Foolish to let her eyes water over something so silly. She blinks hard, turns her attention back to the page, her pencil trembling in the margin: "Why not?" she writes. Why not, indeed.

If she were a man, would she have followed the woman off the train? Making ridiculous stabs at conversation, that inevitably begin with, *Hey, baby!* No. She would follow silently, the way she's always imagined gay men follow each other: predator and prey, each changing sides in the long dance of desire.

Up the escalator to the street, and there she would stop to buy a perfect, blood-red rose from the one-eyed flower vendor on the corner. The woman in the white dress would turn, once only, look over her shoulder to assure herself that Francesca was still there. They would go to a hotel, maybe, or one of those tiny apartments on O'Farrell Street, the kind where rusting "For Rent" signs always hang. The woman in the crocheted dress would live alone, would prick her finger on one thorn. Francesca would lick the blood drop, taste the copper of blood, the salt of skin. There would be no words exchanged. Francesca would call herself Frankie. The woman in the crocheted dress would lie, too. They would not fall in love; they would never see each other again.

Frankie would break the hearts of a hundred women—well, a couple dozen, anyway—and never fall in love again. Frankie wouldn't listen to promises women can't or won't keep. She would know how to play the game. She'd kiss them hard and say, "I don't do love." And they'd understand and not ask for more.

But Francesca McClain is not Frankie. She is a middle-aged woman who teaches freshman English and takes summer vacations to Mexico because it is cheaper than Europe; who has two good pieces of art—her grandmother's silverplate tea service, and a small collection of autographed first edition Steinbecks—which she began collecting after Marlene's abrupt departure. She has not had a date in five years; no one has asked and she wouldn't know where to begin. Or how.

The thought of giving herself up to another woman frightens her, although less than this lonely hunger that threatens to consume her. Complicated as they are beautiful, women are eternal mazes, turning continually inward to the soul. Men must be easier, she imagines, content with their possessions, those things which can be counted, protected, and stored. Women have no such possessions, at least not the kind men value so well. They bring nothing to each other except their selves. Loving women becomes dangerous work, for if what one gives to the other isn't enough, good enough, is tarnished or frayed, shopworn, battered, or too deeply damaged, then what is left? What is left of the selves that is good enough? How amazing that men imagine women love each other because it is easier, instead of the truth: hard as it is, it's the only thing that leaves you whole, the only thing that dissolves the heart, that leaves you liquid in their hands.

Francesca McClain straightens her skirt, puts her book away in her canvas tote bag with the seal of the university emblazoned on its side, and stands up slowly as the train pulls into the station. At the top of the escalator, she will stop and buy a perfect red rose from the one-eyed flower vendor. It will make her late for class. And for the first time in a very long time, she doesn't really care.

PERSIMMON BLACKBRIDGE

Clean

TRUDI-AND-ALLISON'S HOUSE WAS Jam's most boring cleaning job. Probably they didn't tidy up before she came over, probably they just led very clean lives. Jam preferred Sam-and-Tina's because their house was always really dirty without being gross. Gross is cat puke on the carpets and pots left soaking 'til the mold is an inch tall and bizarre creatures lurk in the bottom, farting noxious fumes. Sam-and-Tina's was just sticky floors, bathtub rings: the stuff of exciting scrub work. Trudi-and-Allison's had two bathtubs but no rings, ever. Jam tried to convince herself that her work had meaning. If you dust a shelf that has no dust, you are not wasting your time, you are ensuring it will never *get* dusty. Preventive cleaning, the latest thing.

Allison was always off being a lawyer, but Trudi flitted in and out on her way to and from the university, kissing the air by Jam's cheek as she passed. Only Women Studies' professors air-kiss their cleaning ladies. That's a lie. Only Trudi. She was also the one who introduced Jam to a friend of hers, saying, "She cleans for me sometimes, but her real work is as an artist." The friend nodded to Jam on her knees rubbing at scuff marks on the white tile floor. "I don't know," she said, "that looks like real work to me."

Good line.

Jam kept her head down, hid her smile. Trudi laughed, ha ha ha you're such a card, Alex. There was something in that laugh, something in Alex's remark that smelled of old resentments papered over with politeness. Jam risked a glance. Alex was watching her, ready to share a smirk. Trudi was fussing with her briefcase, anxious to leave. Ex-lovers, definitely. She gave Alex the smirk. Trudi finished fussing and off they went, lunch at the new Italian place. Run by Anglos from Toronto. Jam kept scrubbing—those black scuff marks a certain kind of boot heel leaves. They do come off eventually.

Jam was upstairs making Trudi and Allison's big double bed when she heard the front door open, then close. Then silence. Trudi would have called out, "Hi Jam, it's me!" Allison wouldn't be home in the middle of the day. Footsteps on the stairs. Jam had often wondered what she'd do if a daring daylight burglar broke in while she was working. "Hi, I'm the cleaner. Go ahead and help yourself; just don't make a mess, okay?" But it was probably Trudi. She went out into the hall to check.

Alex.

She stood at the top of the stairs. No "Hi there, I forgot my jacket," no nothing. Just looking at Jam. Jam felt momentarily awkward, then toughened up. She was wearing her Miami Beach t-shirt and dirty jeans with a dust-rag tucked into the back pocket. So what? Alex was wearing something tweedy with subtle leather, looking like a butch professor, which she was. Who cares?

Alex let the silence stretch out a bit longer, then said, "You're still here."

Jam checked her watch. "Two more hours."

"Good."

Silence again. Jam let a slow smile build. Alex came a step closer, another step. Her hand on Jam's cheek, Jam waiting, letting it build, then Alex's mouth on hers, soft lips for a long second, then hard tongue. They stood in the doorway, bodies pressed close, hands everywhere. When the moaning started, Alex led them into the bedroom.

In general, Jam preferred the ambiguity of hallways. But this time it was supposed to be in the bedroom, on the half-made bed. Trudi's bed. It was all about Trudi. Alex wanted to fuck Trudi's cleaning lady.

Jam had never been fucked as someone's cleaning lady before. After seventeen years of cleaning houses it was about time.

There are many reasons to fuck a cleaning lady: her skill, her strength, her beauty. From Alex it was an insult. But the insult was aimed at Trudi. Jam was incidental, nothing, a servant. It was kind of a turn-on to be so invisible. Besides, Jam had her own story. I fucked your ex-lover in your bed. Your university professor ex-lover. She tangled her hands in Alex's sixty-dollar haircut, pulled her head down, bit her mouth. Unbuttoned the tweed thing, the soft leather. Pushed into Alex's cunt slow and sweet, pulled out fast and insolent. Alex liked that. Grabbed Jam's breasts with mean hands, bit her nipples to the edge of pain. Nasty. Someone scratched marks down someone's back. Someone said *give it to me bitch come on.* They struggled on Trudi's bed, did things to each other's bodies until first one and then the other came in great sobbing waves. Then Alex got dressed and left.

All in all it was a pleasant change from preventive dusting. Jam hurried through the rest of her cleaning. Downstairs again, getting her cheque from the kitchen table, Jam noticed new heel marks on the floor. Alex's boots.

TERESA SAVAGE

Pleasing Cleopatra

My LOVER, CLEOPATRA, BROUGHT HOME a slab of solid wax in a tiny aluminum frying pan, complete with an oversized paddlepop stick for stirring. She works in a chemist shop and finds the lure of the products hard to resist.

"Let's give it a whirl," she said. "Who wants fuzzy legs? You first."

I wanted desperately to please Cleopatra. I acquiesced. It involved undressing. She read the directions. I unbuttoned my 501s.

One. Area to be waxed must be clean and dry.

"Have you had a shower today?" Cleopatra can be ruthless. I told her I had.

Two. Place the metal tray on a low heat and leave until two-thirds melted.

She took me by the elbow and steered me to the kitchen, pushing me down on an upturned milk crate. She slammed the pan onto the stove and turned up the gas. Cleopatra meant business.

At this stage, remove from heat source and carefully stir wax using a spoon or the applicator, until its consistency is that of a thick soup.

"Which reminds me," said Cleopatra, "I haven't eaten since breakfast." She pulled a tub of marinated artichoke hearts from the fridge and popped one into her mouth. "Want one?"

Three. Be careful not to have the wax too hot. Test for heat on the back of your hand.

Just like you do with babies' bottles. "Here goes," Cleopatra said, dripping a bobble of wax onto her billowy knuckles. I love her cavalier attitude.

Four. After the melted wax has reached the right consistency and is comfortably warm, apply to the area where the hair is to be removed.

"Show me your leg. Come on, hold it up. I'll fetch a chair to rest your foot on." She disappeared, returning with an ancient footstool, the red velvet padding faded to brown. "It was Aunty Vi's," she said. "She'd be spittin' chips up there if she knew what we were using it for, the old bag. Come on, give me your foot." Cradling my heel in the palm of her hand, she let it slide onto the velvet. "There you go, fit for a queen."

Five. Spread wax about one-eighth of an inch throughout, doing only one strip at a time.

Cleopatra ladled the molten wax onto my proffered limb. She spread it slowly, smoothing it out as lovingly as an old-time plasterer with a trowel full of cement-render. "Do you think that was an eighth of an inch?" she asked. I was only able to pucker a grimace. Luckily Cleopatra thought I was inviting a kiss, and steadying the wax pot on the bench, she took time off to drag her precious lips across my mouth.

Six. As soon as the wax is no longer sticky, and you can leave your fingerprint without the wax sticking to your finger, it must be removed.

"Here goes then," said Cleopatra, "a little pain for the ultimate beauty of smooth, curvaceous legs." She dropped the spatula into the pot and rubbed her palms together.

Seven. Start at one corner and, using a quick, lifting, pulling motion against the growth of hair, remove the entire strip.

Cleopatra curled up the edge of the wax strip, rubbing her thumb against the camber of my shin. She rolled a small amount, a thin white wax snake, enough to grip between her finger and thumb. I shifted on the milk crate.

"Bum's going numb," I said.

"You have to do it quickly," said Cleopatra, tugging hard. Searing pain shot through my shank. Burning. Agonizing. Red hot needles. Pain that leaves a lasting imprint.

Should flecks of wax remain, simply press the back of the newly removed strip against the flecks to remove them.

"Aaagh, Cleopatra, you can't do that," I screamed.

An hour later we are curled up in her bed. Cleopatra wields a pair of delicate nail scissors. With her wide bare back to me, she lifts the last of the clump of wax gingerly, snipping the hairs underneath. I grip her shoulders so tight that my nails excavate her flesh.

"I can't believe all those women who do this all the time," she says, "even their pubes. Can you imagine?"

"No."

"And anyway, what's so wrong with having woolly legs?" she asks.

"Nothing."

"I'm sorry, love, I really am. But it's been an experience anyway, eh?"

Cleopatra is well-known for her intelligence, charm, and wit.

"I'll tell you what," she says. "We've got these great new face masks in the shop, made from real Egyptian mud, straight from the Nile. I might bring us two home tomorrow night. What do you reckon?"

A N N E   S E A L E

My Next Ex

HELLO THERE!" SHE SAYS, with a husky voice.

"Hello yourself," say my hormones, diving into my bloodstream. I tell them to climb out again, because she isn't speaking to me, she seems to have taken a fancy to my buddy Lorraine on the next stool, which is fine with because Lorraine is looking for love, and I am not.

I had had my last relationship. They all end up the same. Badly. It's become a nightmarish pattern. We meet, fall into bed, move in together way too soon, fight more and more frequently, and split up in anger, upsetting all our friends. I have no reason to think it will be any different the next time. Next time? Bite my tongue!

Since she of the husky voice is deep in conversation with Lorraine, there's no danger in looking her over. My hormones didn't lie, she's my type all right, androgynous to the max. Short brown curls on top of a squarish body wearing Levi's low on the hips and, oh no, black motorcycle boots. There *is* danger. I spin to face the bar, giving my undivided attention to the sign posted on the wall across from me—"5 to 7 wing special—20 cents each—mild, medium, or RuPaul."

The song that's been blaring out of the jukebox tapers off, and I hear the husky voice say, "Would you mind introducing me to your friend?"

I glance around in case another of Lorraine's pals has come by, but no, there's no one else. It's me who's being smiled at.

"Uh, sure," Lorraine says. "This is my old friend, Barbara." Is it my imagination or did she emphasize "old"? "Barb, this is L.J."

L.J.? Oh-oh! Three of my ex-lovers went by initials: C.D., K.T. and D.M.V. "Pleased to meet you," I mumble, not looking at her, gazing instead at two tall women who are leaning against the jukebox, pushing buttons. Patsy Cline begins wailing "Crazy."

"Would you like to dance with me, Barbara?" L.J. asks.

"No, thanks," I say. "I don't dance well." Which is the truth.

L.J. presses her leg against mine. "That's because you haven't danced with me. I'm one hell of a leader." She grabs my hand, pulls me off the stool and whirls me into her arms, pressing my body tightly against hers. We move slowly, as one. I must be one hell of a follower.

My mouth is next to her ear. It's either talk or nibble. "So, L.J.," I say, "do you come to this bar often?"

"No. Do you?"

"Once in a while," I lie. Between lovers, I practically live here.

"I just moved from Syracuse," she says. "I got a job at Quaig Electronics."

"Really? I heard Quaig wasn't hiring."

"When you've got skills like mine, everyone's hiring."

I don't know how two bodies crushed as close as ours can produce friction, but on the word "skills," L.J. rubs sideways against me, and no kidding, I see stars. I decide it's time to put my cards on the table, although it would be a lot easier if there were actually a table between us. "I should tell you right now, L.J., I'm not looking for a lover," I say. "In fact, I don't want any more romance in my life, ever."

She stops dead in her tracks, which means of course that I do too, pulls her head back and looks at me, her dark eyes reflecting the strobes. "Why not?"

"It's too complicated. . . ."

"Try me."

The sparkle in her eyes is totally mesmerizing, so I return to the ear. "You see, I don't do well in relationships," I tell it, "and romance leads to relationships."

"It can," she says. I feel her breath in my hair.

"It does," I murmur, sinking into a libidinous fog.

"So you don't ever want another lover . . . ?"

"I don't." Two words in a row seem to be about as much as I can manage at the moment.

"How about another ex-lover?"

"What?"

"How about if we skip the relationship part, and be ex-lovers?" She starts swaying me a bit.

"Why?" I'm down to one-word responses now. All I want is to sink to the floor, bringing her with me.

"Are you on good terms with your exes, Barbara?"

"Some. . . ."

"Have you ever gotten back together with an ex?"

"No."

"Good, then. I'm your ex-lover. No threat."

I wish I could think more clearly. Something tells me this shouldn't be sounding as reasonable as it does. We start moving again, to "I Fall to Pieces." The tall women must really be Patsy fans.

After a while, L.J. says, "Remember how we used to have late suppers in front of the fireplace?"

"Who did?"

"We did, remember? Back when we were together?"

Oh, I see, it's a game. I have no trouble imagining a late supper with her. We're sitting on a thick rug, the smouldering logs providing the only light. "Yes," I say. "I do."

"Remember the way I'd undress you slowly, kissing every part of your body as soon as it came into view?"

"Oh, yes." She must be holding me up. My legs have turned to putty.

"And then I'd take champagne and pour it—" She pauses.

"Where?" I gasp.

"You've forgotten, haven't you?"

"No. Yes."

"Well, since we're exes, I don't think there would be any problem if I refresh your memory by doing it again, do you? For old times' sake?"

I'm beyond answering. She takes my hand and leads me to my stool where I gather my sweater and purse while she orders a bottle of champagne to go.

Lorraine is staring at me in disbelief. "I thought you were all done with romance," she says.

"It was romance with us the first time around, maybe," I tell her. "But now it's just reminiscing. No threat."

The champagne comes. "Back in Baby's Arms," Patsy sings, as L.J. and I leave the bar arm in arm, just like old times.

SHELLY RAFFERTY

Grace Before Sex

I GUESS WE WOKE UP WANTING EACH OTHER but, dumb luck, we'd both overslept. Although her hand had been neatly tucked between my thighs, Grace inadvertently uprooted a few sprigs of my pubic hair as she reached to swat the startling chirp of the alarm clock.

"Yeowww!" I howled, bolting upright.

"Sorry, honey. Better hustle. We're late again."

Her t-shirt hit me in the head as she tossed it off, angled around the corner of the bedroom door, and made a beeline for the shower. I fell back among the pillows and sighed.

I must have drifted off again, because the next thing I knew Grace was jostling me, thereby also sloshing the top of her hot coffee onto my bare thigh. I grimaced.

"Oops," she said hurriedly. "Sorry." She swiped at the growing stain on the sheet. "What are you wearing today?" She set her coffee on top of the bureau and grasped my wrists to haul me up to sitting.

"I don't want to get up."

Grace arched an eyebrow. "Not even negotiable. Today's payday for you, and we've got bills to pay." She stood precariously on one foot, threading the other into her jeans. She wavered a bit before regaining her ground. Coffee next, then hairbrush. She looked good.

From where I sat cross-legged, I opened the top drawer of the dresser and sleepily fished for clean underwear.

"Yikes!" I quickly extracted my hand from the silk boxers and cotton bikinis. Speared on the end of my index finger was an old "Question Authority" button. I snapped my hand and the button fell to the floor, somewhere near the edge of the mattress. I jammed my finger in my mouth to soothe my wounded extremity.

Grace spied the pin and leaned over to collect it. On her way up, she caught the corner of the open drawer on her dangling earring. "Zowie!" she exclaimed, grabbing at the ear. "Do you think it's too early for my Van Gogh imitation?"

"I gather that means you are bloodied but unbowed," I answered, finally swinging my legs over the side of the bed. I knew she wasn't serious. Every bone in my body ached. I dreaded returning to work, where I would spend all day at thirty feet tenuously gripping a rotten ladder to paint the window trim on a monstrous Victorian mansion.

Grace leaned down and kissed my mouth. "Come on, sweetie. Into the drink with you. I left the shower running. . . ." I stood up too quickly and lost my balance.

"Whoa!" Grace reached out to grab me before I kiltered to the floor and we banged our noggins together with the effort. I fell back on the bed dragging Grace on top of me, but not before she stepped on my big toe.

"Are you trying to kill me this morning?" I complained, jerking my knee upward with the bounce of my bedward fall. This action caught Grace squarely in the crotch.

"Unnnhh . . ." she mumbled, tumbling off beside me. We breathed heavily in silence for a moment.

"I find this strangely exhilarating," she said finally, starting to laugh.

"It's not exactly my idea of foreplay," I chuckled.

"Maybe it should be . . ." Grace suggested. She paused and turned to face me. "I have a class in half an hour."

"Ah ha," I said, and rolled over on top of her, unfortunately pinning her long hair under my elbow.

"Ouch ouch ouch ouch ouch!" she said, eyes wide, as I repositioned my arm. "I don't know if I'm more afraid to get out of bed or stay in!"

"Let's just lie here a minute and think this over," I recommended. "You smell good."

"Shampoo," said Grace, slightly shifting under me.

"I think I'm wet," I whispered, suddenly aware of the familiar hot flush between my legs.

"Don't move," said Grace.

"Good idea," I answered.

JOHANNE CADORETTE

The French Trap

SHE'D MADE A BEE-LINE for the cultural studies section, passing all the fun stuff like lesbian fiction and erotica. She didn't even glance up at me, but I noticed her. I've always been a sucker for lanky blondes with crew cuts, coming from a long line of short brunettes myself. Exoticizing the WASP, who would have thought?

It seemed unlikely that some out-of-town theory-head would be interested in picking up a lowly Montréal bookseller. I popped in an Edith Piaf CD for the right touch of solace.

I heard some shuffling at the back of the store. She was heading toward me with a pile of books. She plopped Irigaray, Kristeva, and Foucault down on the counter like some postmodern orgy and boldly said, "Piaf. Good choice."

Bingo. A francofile. And blue eyes to boot.

"She's very wonderfool," I answered, adjusting my speech dial to All-Purpose French Accent. "Zat will be seventy-tree dollars and sirteen cents, please," I continued, brushing a strand of hair away from my face.

She slapped an AmEx Gold card down in front of me. Christy Tucker. Indeed.

"Tell me," said Christy Tucker, holder of an AmEx Gold card, "would you recommend a good place to go out tonight? I'm in town for a conference and I'd like to check out some bars."

"*Voyons.* . . . Today is Friday, no? On Fridays, most of ze girls go out to Le Salon. Don't go zer before eleven, at ze earliest."

"Thank you very much. I'll try that."

Needless to say, I was at Salon by eleven thirty, but there was no sign of Christy Tucker. I sipped a martini and tried to grab Jen, the bartender, for a bit of conversation between clients.

"I swear, Jen, I'm so glad I dropped out of grad school. This chick I'm after spent an hour in the theory section just soaking in all that shit. Foucault! Who needs it? But she makes way more money than I do. I'll never get a gold card. Maybe I should have stuck it out. . . ."

"Excuse me," someone said directly behind me. "I believe you've lost something."

I turned around and faced Christy Tucker. She was dressed classic butch with an edge: crisp white t-shirt, loose jeans, a couple of chunky silver rings, and a thick bathtub chain around her neck. She had an immaculate black leather jacket draped over one shoulder.

"Oh!" I said, startled. "What did I lose?"

"Your accent, you half-wit. Cheers."

She tilted her glass at me and went to sit at a table by herself.

"Shit, I blew it," I said, downing the last of my drink.

"Nah," said Jen, wiping the counter. "Walk past her and go up to the bathroom. What can it hurt?"

Salon is not the most happening dyke bar in town, but it has beautiful, clean bathrooms with stall doors and walls that go right down to the floor. I sashayed my mini-skirted butt right past her and headed for the stairs. I briefly turned around to see if she was looking. She wasn't.

I bolted myself into one of the cubicles, figuring I might as well make use of it. I had just finished when someone entered the bathroom and didn't make any noise for about twenty seconds. There was a knock on my door.

I pulled my skirt down over my garter.

"Occupied!"

"Open up, little French girl," came the response.

I froze momentarily and opened the door. Christy Tucker.

"*Quelle surprise*," I said, looking right into her eyes.

"Shut up," she replied, soflty pushing me against the wall.

She began to kiss my neck, while her hands roamed my body. Finding the bare skin between my stockings and my panties, she smiled appreciatively and moved her fingers higher. I was very, very wet.

"You want this?" she asked.

I nodded.

"Good. But tell me in French."

She slipped a finger inside my underwear and felt the wetness. I moaned and she took it away.

"Say it in French," she repeated.

Oh well. Here goes.

"Fourre moi."

"That's good," she said, pulling my underwear down.

She rubbed her hand against my clit. I shuddered.

"That feel good?"

"Oui, oh oui," I answered dutifully.

She unzipped my top, leaving my breasts exposed. She bent down and licked my hard nipples.

"Oui. N'arrête pas," I urged her, putting one foot on the toilet.

"Say 'You're driving me crazy,'" she ordered, rubbing my clit quickly now.

I could hardly speak, but I managed to say, *"Tu me rends folle."*

"Say 'I want you so badly.'"

"Je te veux tellement."

She slowly penetrated me, first with one, two, and later I lost count how many fingers. I was so wet I could have taken more. She moved in and out of me with a delectable, deliberate slowness.

"Fuck me, baby."

"Fourre moi, bébé."

"I'm on fire with desire."

"*Je brûle de* . . ."

She was fucking me forcefully now, and I gasped.

"Finish it!"

I couldn't. Her fingers were deep inside of me, pumping in and out. Her thumb grazed my clit and I moaned loudlly.

"Yes!"

She stopped.

"In French, you slut!"

Fuck!

"Oui!"

She resumed, harder now, quicker. My legs were turning to jelly and it seemed that my juice was all over the place, on my legs, hers, the floor. I closed my eyes and let myself get lost in this incredible sensation. I was close to coming and she sensed it. She fucked me faster.

"Are you going to come for me?"

"Oui, je vais jouir pour toi," I whispered.

"Louder!" she commanded, grabbing my ass with her other hand and pulling me closer. Her other hand went deep inside me.

"Je jouis! Oh, oui . . . oui!!"

My entire body shook and I came, collapsing against the wall.

Someone knocked on the door. We looked up at each other, shocked.

"Ostie les filles, j'ai envie! Avez-vous fini?!"

TONYA YAREMKO

To Stanley Park

IT'S A BEAUTIFUL SUNDAY AFTERNOON and I'm stuck in the dining room of an upscale law office in downtown Vancouver. My girlfriend is busy washing the heap of dishes the overpaid lawyers have left for her. Waiting, I sit back in a well-cushioned easy chair and flip eagerly through the pages of Ann Bannon's *I Am a Woman*. I am incredibly, unmistakably, horny.

I make my way into the kitchen area. My girlfriend is bent over washing down the cupboards. Her round ample ass looms in my face. A vision of her doing the exact same act minus the clothing lodges itself firmly in my mind. I gasp. She turns, looks up and sees in my eyes a sexual hunger which always throws her off balance.

"Hi, honey. What's up?" She stands.

Slowly, I approach, lean forward then quickly lick the side of her neck. "I'm horny," I say, rubbing my breast against hers.

"No! No! No!" she turns, walks away from me, toward her small office in the back. In her office she searches frantically for excuses. Am I crazy? This is her work site. There are security cameras everywhere. At the thought of security cameras my sex becomes wetter. It's a law firm. She'd be fired.

"Hell," I think to myself, "I'm always up for a bit of lesbian activism." I drape my hot pink t-shirt over a nearby chair and begin to squeeze my nipples and rub my breasts.

My girlfriend is appalled. "Put that back on!"

I sit on a chair. "I need you to fuck me."

"Not here," she groans, struggling between her proper British upbringing and her rising sexual passion. She loves it when I assert myself. "How about we go to the park? Stanley Park."

I shake my head. I'm beginning to sweat. I stand, move in front of her and wrap my arms around her neck. "Fuck me, baby. Fuck me now."

She pulls me close, kisses me hungrily.

Fifteen minutes later, hair tousled, she turns away trying, once again, to gain control.

"This is crazy. I'm going to get fired."

My clit is swollen, aching for her touch. Moving closer to her I tear open my jeans, grasp her hand and slide it in. Her fingers, having a will of their own, begin rubbing and searching.

"God—sweetheart—someone—will come in."

"Just a quickie, lover. Just a quickie."

My legs are buckling. Her lips are all over me. I begin to writhe. Whimpers, low at the base of my throat, rise to high-pitched cries.

"Shhh. Try to be quiet."

Quiet! Quiet? Never in all our lovemaking have I ever been quiet. As far as I'm concerned getting fucked and being quiet are oxymoronic. I am not only a moaner and a groaner, but one hell of a screamer.

"Damn it, woman!" she exclaims, sweeping me into her arms and laying me onto the floor.

My naked back arches against the carpet. Her strong, fast hands stroke me. She pulls down my jeans, trapping my legs. One, two, three fingers plunge inside me. Searching, teasing, fucking me. That's it—I start to scream.

"This is crazy. You're crazy." Panting, she grabs my t-shirt and stuffs it into my mouth. My body twitches and twists in satisfaction. Juices gush out of me. She goes down. There is nothing, nothing in the world right now, but her head between my legs, licking, slurping, eating me. Heaven is a law office in downtown Vancouver.

Two hours later she helps me into my clothes. Looking at me, awed and exasperated, she shakes her head.

"Quickie, my ass!"

Together we laugh. In power. In joy. In triumph. Then, my activism done for the day, we leave, initiating our trek to Stanley Park.

T. J. BRYAN

Telephone Strip at Bedtime

TWELVE MIDNIGHT. YOU SHOULD BE HOME from your shift by now. I key in your telephone number and wait. On the third ring you pick up. "Yeah, hello?"

"You busy?"

"Nope. Wha's up?"

"Woman, I'm so *hot* for the feel of your lips on my clit I can't work. Can't think straight. Can't sleep."

"Oh yeah?"

"Unh-hunh. What're you gonna do about it?"

"Me?" You're *toyin'* with me now. "Tell me, little girl, *what* does *your* drippin' pussy have to do with me?"

"It's all your fault." This juice pumpin' relentlessly outta my snatch, slicked on the insides of my thighs. The way my nipples are still tender from the merciless torture they received from your teeth. That my ass is still throbbin' and tender from the spankin' you gave me this morning. That my lips are still cravin' the taste of your cunt.

More laughter from you. "*And? So?* I *tole* you I can't leave the house tonight—"

"Hush—I under*stand* you've got responsibilities. For what *I'm* gonna do you won't *have* ta leave your house."

"Oh yeah? But—"

"Shhh—just lay back, baby and get comfortable."

There are a few seconds of movement and rustling on your end, then you give me the go ahead. "A'right sweet thang, sock-it-ta-me."

One of my hands plays gently across my hardened nipples. A long, low-pitched moan escapes my lips. Then I whisper, "I wanna *please* you—in every conceivable way. But first I wanna show you what I've got to *give*." I turn on the radio and let the smooth, liquid sounds of B.L.K.'s "Quiet Storm" envelope me and you in some serious come-suck-me music. There's a sista singin', singin' 'bout all the different ways she can please her daddy. She's got this sulky, pouty l'il girl voice. And in between verses she makes my pussy hairs stand on end with her sexy sighs.

She lets loose with a moan so intense I feel it between my thighs. My eyes roll back in my head and I say, "I wanna dance for you. Close you eyes, daddy. Can you see me? I'm wearin' a skin-tight, sheer, stretchy, black lace mini-dress. This dress is *so* sheer. Do you know how sheer it is, hon?"

You breathe in deeply and exhale. "Fuckin' slut. How sheer is it?"

"Well—it's so sheer you can just about see my hard nipples over the red lace demi bra I'm wearin'. But look lower. What do you see?"

Gettin' into the game, you say, "It's hard to see you in this light. Why don't you tell me?"

"Matching red high-cut lace briefs. And they're soaked."

"Oh, yeah?"

I stretch out on my bed, careful not to drop the telephone receiver. With my other hand I trace a lazy path past my well-rounded belly to my cunt. "Yeah—and I've got on garters and stockings too."

You inhale sharply. "Fuck. You *know* how a woman in stockings and garters makes me hard, clit-tease."

I giggle, excited by the knowledge that I've pushed the right button.

"So?" you say. "Tell me more about this dance you're doin'."

"We're at the bar. Though you're seated well away from the stage, you're the only customer I notice. I start off slow, proud of my curves, my height, and my grace. I allow my hands to roam over my body. My long legs flex and bend as my body writhes, flowing in time with the music. I turn away from the crowd, place my gloved hands on the wall behind me and bend over, causing my dress to ride up. Offering you a clear view of my panties and ass, I look back and catch your eye to make sure you know this is for *you*. *Only* for you."

Still careful to hold onto the receiver, I begin rubbing the smooth skin of my breasts and belly with my other hand. On your end of the line I hear you cussin' softly under your breath. I know you're playin' with yourself.

"Slowly, sinuously I bring myself back into an upright position. And roll my hips and butt, undulating and peaking like waves crashing on the rocks of a jagged coastline. I close my eyes and let the bass replace the beating of my heart. I become one, pure, fleshy, ebony note playing for your pleasure. For your ears alone. Can you hear me, Daddy?"

"Yes, little girl. Can *feel* you too."

"Watch me, lover. I'm grabbing the hem of the dress and drawing it up, past my hips, past my tits and over my head. I stand in front of you in my bra, panties, stockings, and garterbelt. I spread my legs and take turns thrusting my breasts and pussy out toward you. I put my hands behind my back, hold them there, as if you have tied them. I swing low, bending at the waist so the cleft between my breasts is emphasized. Do you want more?"

"Bitch, don't fuck wit' me now. Keep goin'."

"Testy, testy aren't we? Well how 'bout this? I plant my legs firmly beneath me. The way I'm movin' it looks like you're fuckin' me good. Thrustin' your long, black strap-on in and out of me *hard*. My hands release and thumbs hook into the red lace of my panties, ripping them off. Bringin' the thick hairs of my cunt into view."

"I want your legs wrapped around my face," you growl.

"Oh yeah?"

"My tongue wants to get wit' your clit."

"Baby . . . my story's not done yet. Don't worry, the next time I see you, I'll give up the pussy. But right now touch *yours* for me. I wanna know how wet this is making you. Put your fingers in your mouth."

"Uh-huh . . ."

" . . . and suck that juice from me, baby. Suck it! Now, close your eyes and let me dance for you . . . let my body weave and rock. Watch my temperature rise. Watch me lose my breath just *thinkin'* 'bout you. See me try and relieve some of the pressure between my legs by rotating my hips and stompin' my legs in time with the music. Both my arms are raised, they're beckoning you forward, enticing you with fluid motion. You leave your seat and begin to make your way toward me. My body responds with frantic movement. Finally you're with me, next to the stage. With a toss of your head and a flash of your huge, beautiful brown eyes you motion me to move closer. I obey. You remove a bill from your wallet and tuck it into my bra. I allow you to take liberties with the silky smoothness of my breasts that I would castrate another patron for even thinkin' about. Then you slide your hand down my body 'til you reach the dripping, molten, misbehavin' wetness of my hole. I grind myself into your hand and whisper, 'It's yours.' You force a few fingers up into me and use them to pull me closer. The sharp edges of your teeth claim one of my ears. In the midst of ecstatic pain I hear you say, 'Yeah, the pussy is mine.'"

There are short, incoherent grunts on your end of the line. Deep intakes of breath.

"Fuckin' cunt. Ahhh . . . yeah, fuck."

I egg you on, my voice sing-songin', "Oooh yeah, Daddy, come for me. Suck me. Suck me, Daddy. You *know* this cunt belongs to you, don' cha? C'mon, work dat pussy for me."

"Awwfuck. Shit. Suck—muthafuckin—aaannnhhh." Then all I hear is the uneven sound of your breathing.

"You okay, baby?" I ask.

The intensity and hunger in your voice has been replaced with sleep and satisfaction. "Yeah, hon. Just worn out, is all. That was sweet. Gotta . . . mmm . . . sleep now. Call me . . . t'morrow?"

"Tomorrow morning? Sure. You *know* my day doesn't start off right unless I hear your voice. Go to sleep, okay?"

I hang up the receiver to the sounds of you mumbling and snoring softly. Mission accomplished, I wrap myself in my comforter and turn out the light.

ANNA NOBILE

Greatest Strength

I'VE GOT A BIRTHDAY SURPRISE FOR YOU. I hope you like it." Those words ring hollow now, ten days after the fact. She watched you all through the days leading up to the big one when you'd turn thirty. She never let on, never gave anything away, not even after you just came right out and asked her: *when?*

On the big day, if your friends hadn't made a fuss over you, it would have passed like any other day.

"Ho-hum. Dinner and a movie. How predictable," she scoffed mildly.

Then she climbed on top of you, pushed up the sides of your mouth to force a smile. When you didn't co-operate, she ripped your shirt open, sent buttons flying, licked and pinched your nipples; nipples that are your greatest strength. Like flicking little marbles, they send beams of pleasure through your body, hitting the willing target of your clitoris. Your greatest strength, your greatest weakness. You forget about sulking and let her take you to that place where birthdays don't matter.

Tonight though, as you head for the bar, you can't help feeling a little resentful. Ten days later, and still no surprise.

The bar is unusually dim as you step through the door. Music blares. The place sounds packed. But when you round the corner, the dance floor is empty. You look around, but there isn't a soul anywhere. Stepping out onto the floor you crane your neck, trying to spot the deejay. The booth also looks empty.

A spotlight comes on, blinding you. Then another and another. You put your hand to your eyes, but all you can see are silhouettes of women standing in a perimeter around the dance floor. A husky voice starts singing. *Her* voice, sticky as melting marshmallows. "Happy Birthday to you. Happy birthday, dear lover. Happy birthday to you." She says, "I've got a surprise for you. Hope you like it."

The silhouettes are upon you like a swarm of bees protecting their queen. They remove your clothes, stinging you with pinches and bites, and lay you on the centre of the cold dance floor. The mirrored ball turns above you, reflecting back in fragments the shattered lights of a new world. The music starts up again and you recognize the song she plays to get you out of your long, silly sulks. You wanted your surprise, begged for it. Well, here it is at last.

Ropes are tied to your hands and feet, your limbs spread wide as the binds are pulled taut, stretching and pulling you with them. Pinpoints of light illuminate your breasts, your labia fall open naturally from the position you now find yourself in. You realize you have been laid bare for all to see. Anyone can do anything they like to you at any moment, and there isn't a thing you can do about it.

You look, but can't see her, the one in charge, the queen bee.

The leather ends of a cat o' nine tails hover above your face, descend onto your waiting lips. You breathe in; a smell of leather and sex envelopes you as the tails are pulled slowly along, the ends licking your nipples, slapping your belly. Hands caress your legs, pull on your toes, explore your inner thighs. Little pools form in the folds of your cunt, but no one seems to notice, no one seems to care. They're too busy exploring your skin.

A woman with bright red lipstick kneels by you and massages your head. Every part of you tingles, alive with sensation. You want to kiss this woman, strain for her, but you can only squirm, encouraging the silhouettes to tease you more and more. The lipsticked woman senses your need, holds her lips that smell like chocolate just within reach, so you nibble away, trying to satisfy your hunger. Someone is making exploratory licks around the fine folds of your labia just at the moment that someone else begins sucking your nipple. You gush just enough to dribble onto the floor. There is an appreciative moan. Yours or someone else's? You can't tell anymore.

You want to return the touch—someone's, anyone's. You tug on the ropes in vain. Someone offers you a dildo, and taking it full into your mouth you suck, grateful for anything that will give you something to do. The pinching of your nipples continues, the caressing of every part of your body does not cease, the licking around your clit and the opening of your vagina becomes more certain. Your juices spill out onto the floor.

"Now! Now, oh yes, now!"

Everything stops.

She stands naked above you. You can see her clit peeking through her pubic hair. With her fingers she spreads herself to give you a better view, kneels, settling on your mouth. She's not even upon you before you begin licking and prodding her.

She moves onto your stomach.

"I love my surprise," you whisper.

"I haven't given it to you yet," she says.

She swabs your left breast with something cold and wet. The smell of rubbing alcohol reaches you. Your nipple springs to attention, and before you have a chance to put it all together, the thing is done. She has pierced your nipple.

The pain courses through your body. Tears spring to your eyes. You pull weakly on your ropes. She pierces the other nipple. Your greatest strength, your greatest weakness.

Her tongue feels its way to your hard clit and begins the motions that you so longed for when your nipples were still whole. The endorphins kick in. You stop crying long enough to enjoy the moment you know will never come again.

MIRIAM CARROLL

A Night Out

VICKI SEARCHED ACROSS THE DANCE FLOOR, her eyes piercing the semi-darkness and maze of decibels. There. She spotted the woman again, dancing in a group of three. Vicki was attracted to the way she moved: slowly, in the midst of all the writhing bodies, sensuously taking advantage of her slight obesity by accenting the movement of thighs, ass, and stomach in her dance. The woman's long dress was well-chosen to compliment her full figure, swaying with each movement.

Vicki had come to the dance at her friend Sal's prodding, to get them both out of the solitary pattern they seemed to have fallen into. Sal giggled that they were both hungry for a date, and Vicki had to agree. Vicki chose to wear her sexy leather outfit. Might as well do it right, she thought.

Now Vicki ambled around the edge of the floor, avoiding the flailing arms and legs of the dancers. She wanted a closer look at this lovely lady, maybe catch her eye. The heavy beat finally caught her. Unconsciously, she started keeping their rhythm, dancing by herself, until she worked her way to the triad, and joined in. The three became four, then two, as Vicki cut the woman off from her companions with a disarming smile and unspoken words.

The interminable song finally wound down. Vicki, perspiring, said, "Whew, would you like to go out and cool off?"

"Sure. You are a good, smooth dancer. I like your style."

Off to a good start, Vicki mused. Back through the crowds they went, finding a seat in the vestibule. It was quieter there. Vicki took in closely the face of the woman. She had a round, moon face, narrow nose dividing the centre. Her lips were full, kissy lips, bright red lipstick exactly applied. She smiled as she sat down, spreading out on the bench. Vicki noted her teeth were cat-like, surprisingly small and sharp; her eyes, almost almond-shaped, were pools of inky darkness.

"I'm Vicki. What's your name?"

The woman looked down, clasping her hands. "I'm Soma."

"That's an odd name. I bet everyone says that," Vicki prodded, hoping for an explanation.

"It is an ancient name, Greek, referring to a mystical fluid of the body," Soma explained.

Vicki wasn't much enlightened, and vowed to research it later on.

Soma continued, "I've had it with this crowd. I should go back to the hospital and finish my work there."

Vicki was intrigued, as Soma knew she would be. "Hey, don't leave me like that. What do you do?"

Soma sighed. "I knew you'd ask. I'm a pathologist at Grady's morgue. I study post-mortem—er—blood samples after they're extracted from a corpse. One is waiting for me."

"Well, it can't be in too much of a hurry," Vicki said. She felt drawn to this Soma with the gruesome occupation. "Can I watch?"

Soma smiled her cat smile. "If you can stand the smell of formaldehyde and the sight of blood, shot-up corpses, masks and gloves, it's okay. I'm head of the department."

Vicki was smugly pleased to be accepted into a real inner sanctum.

"I'll be just a minute. I want to tell Sal I'll be having an experience I won't forget for a while," she said, grinning.

They drove to the hospital, chatting about their lives, getting familiar with each other. Vicki felt Soma getting familiar with her knee. She made no move to stop her.

The deserted hallway echoed their footsteps. Soma unlocked the door to her area, handing Vicki a set of sanitary clothes, as they entered the locker room. "You've got to be sterile. Take off your clothes."

Vicki did as she was told. Soma undressed close to her, taking in her shape with eyes, then hands. "That body can wait. This body needs you," she whispered, kissing Vicki's neck. Vicki responded, hands moving down the large body, holding on to the folds of Soma's behind.

This was more than Vicki could ever hope for. She would have settled for the cadaver's blood, cold and dead. But this temptation was more than she could resist.

She turned aside Soma's head with a vicious thrust of her neck, and sank her teeth into the throbbing carotid artery. Soma, paralyzed with terror, didn't even scream.

DELIA SCALES

Cruising

THE CRICKET'S ARMS WAS OVER-FLOWING, the crowd hemorrhaging out over the pavement on a hot February night. A cool breeze picked up the festive voices and tossed them with snatches of disco music over the darkening skyline. Kinetic bodies danced to reveal patches of burnt skin, still stinging from the Sydney sun. Unable to find a park close by, Vivienne and Jackie piled out of their car, leaving Bren to circle the back streets of Surrey Hills.

Like a time warp of Australian pubs in the fifties, the front bar was full of men shouting for rounds of beer and making quick deals, while women jammed the saloon, clinging to tight-knit groups of long-standing friendships. As Bren joined the others, she pulled out a small brown bottle from her pocket, unscrewed the top and sniffed deeply. Vivienne watched indifferently, her own particular drug awaiting her amid the crowd.

Together the three women forced themselves upon the crowd's fluid circumference. As the smell of washed and perfumed women's bodies intoxicated Vivienne, the crowd finally broke open, then just as quickly closed in around them.

"Two schooners and a bourbon and coke," yelled Vivienne over the crush at the bar. While she was waiting, her eyes slowly ran over leather jackets and strong bodies underneath shirts.

"Crowded tonight," remarked Jackie, as she sipped her coke through a straw. Her waist-length brown hair sashayed back and forth over her silk shirt as she warded off appreciative glances toward her good-looking lover. The object of her affections, Bren, said little while downing beer continuously, eyes diluted, her boyish figure agitated in white jeans and short-sleeved shirt.

As salty stains ran down necks, saturated bras, drew patterns on damp backs and shamelessly reached between the legs of the crowd, it became a sexual animal, moving as one. The hot breath of the animal was hungry, eyes searching for someone to spend the night with, arms reaching out for possible victims: a hydra of lust. Long after the staff had forced the crowd out and closed the pub, it prowled the pavement, the hot vacuum of an airless night driving it wild, rage exploding, glasses smashing on the pavement. Bren was dragged away from an impending fight, possessed by the mindless rage of a Saturday night.

Fleeing down suburban back streets, fingers of a Prussian blue shadowy monster snatched at the car as it clung to the security of street lights. It continued bravely on, driving deeper into the jungle of Sydney's gay scene, the city lights surrounding them, chanting a savage sexual rhythm. They drove from bar to bar, as Vivienne searched for love in nightclubs with no names under the sparkle of Oxford street lights. Wading through the litter of drinks, lonely middle-aged women and couples seeking extramarital affairs, she finally settled on an unattached butch woman with trademark short hair and leather jacket. Bren and Jackie left her to enjoy the night, Jackie drunk and sentimental, Bren hyper and agro from fights and amyl nitrate. Vivienne sat silently in the stranger's car as they drove to another house in an anonymous suburb.

As her shirt was pulled back and bare flesh stroked with a hand and then a tongue, she felt both repulsed and deeply sexual. Her faded jeans were tugged off and she sank back on to the bed, her clitoris aching with hunger. The stranger smelled of alcohol as she lay on top of Vivienne, mumbling how beautiful she was, mouth finding mouth, hand finding cunt. At times Vivienne looked around at the furniture, the curtains, posters on the wall. At times the stranger found the right moment and swept her away to a strange place, full of monsters and uncontrollable desires that made her scream in fear as much as pleasure. This is the way it's meant to be, Vivienne told herself as she lay back, looking up at the unfamiliar ceiling, occasionally wincing with pain. This is who I am.

On the journey back to Newcastle, rich apricot sunlight streamed in through the windows. As the train rattled across the broad Wye River, the steel blue water returned the sky's fickle moods with steady reflection.

"Love me," a voice blurted out inside Vivienne, as they approached the scrubby terra vert bush on the other side. "I want someone to hold me, someone to understand me."

Back at art school on Monday, straight people would ask what she'd done on the weekend.

"Nothing much," she'd smile blandly, then seek out her best friend.

"Score, maybe, seven out of ten," she'd boast.

"You gays don't waste any time," Desley would admonish, and Vivienne would shrug carelessly, steal a cigarette, and they'd go back to discussing Michelangelo.

TATIANA BARONA DE LA TIERRA

True Cunt Stories

THE FIRST TIME I HAD REAL, OFFICIAL lesbian sex I fooled my suitor, a seasoned dyke whom I'd trailed secretly and incessantly, until she led me to her king-size waterbed. All it took was a 3 a.m. moonlit skinny dip in a cold lake, a few hits of marijuana, and decades of desire. I was hers, a twenty-one-year-old instant fuck, a fresh groovy girl aching to be indoctrinated. At the time I had a boyfriend with a big dick I enjoyed fucking, an engineer student who liked to wear black lace panties and pretend he was a she. I moaned and rolled on that bed with fake satin sheets, as she fingered my clit and watched me. By sunrise I was a man-hating-lesbian and a witch-in-the-making. Finally.

Along with my new-found freedom I discovered an incredible knack for good sex and sick relationships. That first one, with big white freckled breasts and a collection of long, split-ended hairs, got out quick. She liked the chase and the hot hand work, but those psychic visions of the bratty bitch in bloom sent her scurrying.

Ditched and dedicated to keeping my pussy in action, I cast a spell to attract another lover. She literally knocked on my door, a hazel-eyed tomboy with a wide tongue and long inner lips. She was new in town and she liked getting high and eating me. I liked being eaten and delving into her firm rosy tits and mysterious past. The only problem, as I would reluctantly discover, was that she was a budding psychopath. After a few Charles Manson transformations that ended with frantic 911 calls to the police, I moved out of town, far from her clutches.

My cunt, along with the rest of me, was just beginning to wake up. No matter what I did, one of my priorities was getting it touched and filled and talked to. I went to extremes to fulfill my mission and continued to fuck and emotionally entangle myself with a variety of women. One was a tall jock, flat chested and hairy with a girlie laugh, solid biceps, and enchanting musky pits. The only way she could come was by grinding ferociously on my knuckles, upside down. I could deal with that, but not with her ex-lover who monitored and hounded us and who, eventually, won her back.

Then there was the lumberjack separatist who scrutinized my every move, kissed me with blackberry lips, and chilled me with her sour anger. Another one, even angrier, was an alcoholic artist, a burly top who handcuffed me to a New York City street sign and fucked me right there in the springtime. One night she opened her wide legs and defences and let me fist-fuck her. She stole my grandmother's emerald ring, drank a gallon of Chivas, and claimed my only leather jacket as her trophy.

There was another alcoholic, a seemingly sophisticated, long-legged, and frightened being who taught me that not all photographers are creative. She wouldn't eat my wet pussy or any other slimy thing, and she was such a loser and a lousy fuck that I became frigid. Another one was an adventurous separatist and musician who stole from stores. She had long brown hair that graced the crack of her sweet copper ass and fucked me with a French accent. I wrote her a song that I never sang to her.

A few really loved me. One showered me with sushi and Godivas and fulfilled my every wish. Another drew me with her pain and her real-woman-with-curves-and-swollen-pussy games. Another one, the sweetest of all, put playful elves on my pillow and left a trail of sparks with every step.

A few transformed me. One challenged my racial identity as she gave me every piece of her full-womanly-soft butch body. She would ram me with any object within her reach and when we broke up she threw Greek cucumbers at me, the same ones she fucked me with, from her ninth-story apartment. She had a delicious charcoal silk ass. Another one made me talk during sex in proper Spanish and taught me dramatic sexual technique. She penetrated every single mystery, even the ones I didn't know about, and let me be her little girl and womanly whore in the same breath. She made me cry, she fucked me so good. Another one took me a step further when she made me lick her strap-on dick and then let me suck her shamefully hardened nipples. She hated being a woman, and I loved her for letting me in on her secret.

O D E T T E   A L O N S O

Queen of Hearts

IT'S ALL ALEJANDRA GUZMÁN'S FAULT. Because when my mother came in, crying my name aloud and in horror, it was Alejandra who was moving my hand and my thoughts.

It started a few days before the concert. I wanted to be there and sit right at the front, so she could see me. I was certain she would notice me and, who knows, she might stretch out her hand and I might touch her.

Oh, God, touch Alejandra, have her close to me. That was my chance, my only chance, but nobody would go with me. The ticket was too expensive. I figured we could buy chewing gum at the Central de Abastos and sell it in the subway. But nobody would buy our chewing gum in the subway, much less if we weren't blind or if we didn't cause pity.

Nobody loves Alejandra as Maricela and I do. Although others stare at her every time they see her image on the front covers, none of them trembles at listening to her voice or at watching her on TV.

Maricela and I'd waited for the concert for months. We dreamed about it. But our mothers said they would never give us the money.

"That little woman, Madonna, and Gloria Trevi are of the same disgusting kind," they say.

What a comparison. They also say that they mislead youth to the wrong path. Our mothers cannot explain how those women can be on TV.

"And the way she dresses and the way she dances . . ." my mother says.

What I like most about Alex—honestly—is the way she dresses and dances.

Then Maricela and I told our mothers about the chewing gum and everything got worse. Two girls, brought up by decent families, playing to be beggars just to see that four-letter woman. Maricela and I were confined to our rooms. What's worse, my mother said that it would be better not to see Maricela again because it was a most inconvenient friendship, and her influence over me was negative.

I've never understood grown-ups. According to them, you're not supposed to go around with boys because they're bad, perverse, and they only want to take advantage of you. But now my mother says that I shouldn't go around with girlfriends. And she doesn't tell me why. It seems that all the fuss around Alex's concert is only an excuse to say that Maricela and I aren't great friends. I wonder how she can know how good my friends are. Nobody seemed to notice when Ed, the electrician, in our own living room, showed his erect part to me, forced me to rub it, and made me suck the whitish fluid that came from there. Nobody seemed to hear all his threatenings if I thought to denounce him.

That's why nothing was new to me when boys came to my body. That is why I wasn't even surprised when Vince and I kissed each other and I felt his part pushing. He was my boyfriend and my mother wasn't aware of it. Now I think that I wasn't so sure he was my boyfriend, maybe because he also got into our living room, as if we were studying or watching , and started kissing me. He used to kiss me long, and then he touched my breasts. Then he would pass his hands under my blouse, go down, and caress me there much, fondly, long. I knew I shouldn't enjoy it because that was not decent, but I let him continue. I also let him take his part out and rub it against my part, sometimes with violence. At other times we would lay on the sofa, and he would lay on me. But I never let him go much further. Until one night while everyone was at home watching TV in the study, he was trying to convince me—with the best of his endearments—to go to his place the following day. I said no. I was a decent girl and I should not visit a man alone, because that was not right. And he would fondle the insides of my thighs, so softly I felt a tickle all over me. The more I said no, the more his hand moved upward. I think that I refused so that I would feel his hand very close to my hair and his mouth closing softly over mine. I don't remember how long that lasted because, suddenly, I lost all will to reject him. I let him press me against the wall. I felt my legs being raised to the level of his waist, and his member getting in me without the least trace of resistance or pain.

For the next few months the scene was repeated many, many times. I always said no at the beginning, I think to raise the excitement, but I finally let him do as he pleased. Alejandra showed up later and everything began to change. Vince lost importance: he always wanted the same, and I needed something new.

Kissing Maricela was really new. I, who loved Alejandra, kissed Maricela. Maricela and I loved her so much, so many dreams and fantasies we shared, that kissing came easily. Kissing each other like thirst, like hunger. For Maricela and I, loving Alejandra meant devouring our own mouths and touching each other, as if we were actually touching her. Since then, I dreamed about Maricela's lips on Alex's body, or about Alex's lips on Maricela's body, or about the three of us playing around and kissing each other over an immense bed covered by silk, dark blue sheets, and many pillows.

In the middle of this dream, I go to this town. The grass is a green lichen and the water forms narrow streams. My shoes get wet, and we play in the mud. We're on a gondola or an Old West-movie carriage. No, no. It's a wooden carriage, or maybe it's a turn-of-the-century car, and I help in pushing it because it's stuck in the mud.

She's inside the car wearing a 1900s' dress, then suddenly we're in a room and the voices of men fixing the car come from outside. The light is brilliant, almost blinding, and I don't know if it's her or me or somebody else who, face down, is on the bed. A bodyless hand touches the naked being. I see the hand in the air, and the buttocks, the space between the buttocks. The face I see on the bed is Alejandra's, but it's inside of me that I feel the hand under the body, rubbing faster time after time. My body is the one that is pressed to the bed, crushing the hand, almost paralyzing it. My body is the one that feels the flare approaching, slowly and deeply down from the belly. My body is the one that sees Alejandra's face, the one that feels itself stuck to the hand, and my brain exploding in the very moment that my mother cries in horror. And I awake.

Translated by Elena Madrigal.

MARY MIDGETT

Brunch with Sharon

BLUE SKY. HINTS OF GREY. Hot sun.

After brunch we wash dishes and prepare for a leisurely afternoon. We decide to stay home and enjoy this rare October sunshine. Our minds working simultaneously, we peel off our morning attire. I continue taking off my clothes while Sharon climbs into the deck chair beside me. Finished, I put on my sunglasses and move over to Sharon who is laying on her back, offering her hairy mound to the sun goddess, her breasts surrendering, nipples erect.

I sit on the edge of Sharon's chair, sweat trickling down my face, as I open the tube of sun tanning lotion number #2.

"This lotion is not for black folks," Sharon says. "Where did you get it?"

Feeling foolish, because I thought it was for us folks, I tell her I got it from Avon.

She smiles and says, "Oh well, they are trying."

I grin, squeeze a small amount of oil in the palm of my hand and with my left hand, put some on my fingers. Starting with Sharon's forehead I smooth oil on her, moving slowly and gently over her face until she is a mask of oil. The weather woman just announced the temperature is eighty degrees.

I straddle Sharon, pussy to pussy, put lotion on my palm, rub both hands together to even out the oil, rub Sharon's shoulders, arms, muscles. I massage, touch, and cuddle her breast, her nipples. I raise one to my lips, kiss, lick.

Unstraddling my sweetheart, I lotion her stomach, pussy, legs. Sharon's brown, sleek body resembles a seal emerging from the water, wet, shiny, slippery.

She says to me in a whisper, "Come sit on me again." I mount her like a horse getting ready for the race. I steady myself, moving into position, cunt to cunt, place myself on her forest; it tickles my clitoris, exciting me. I jockey on her pussy and position myself for the ride. Legs into position. I shudder in anticipation of the pleasure to come. The hot sun blazes.

I ride my lover, slowly, softly. We have all the time in the world.

SHARON NOBLE

When the Fat Lady Sings

I CLOSE MY EYES: the sensation is too much. Her hot breath creates a cool, tingly feeling as she suckles my breast. Mmmm . . . oh God! I feel my vaginal walls contracting, a thick filmy liquid collecting at its door. The boy in her is strong and aggressive, drawing out all of my feminine mystique, but for the moment I'm still in control. As I straddle her body, holding her head close to my chest, I can only think in anxious anticipation of my turn. Meanwhile, I take what I want. On my knees, I rise up off of her and slide down onto our toy. There's no limit to what we can do in lust or love, to bring ourselves joy. Tongue sliding up and down from my stomach to my chest, I hear the pleasure she feels and I know she's loves me. Moisture collecting on her shoulders as I balance myself, lets me know just how good it really is for her. Her body rises to meet mine, shoving deeper what now feels like an extension of her love. I can't help but want to reciprocate. Her pace picks up and I return the favour, listening and responding to her nasty words of pleasure. Before I reach my peak, I call out her name. Like a volcanic eruption we both let go.

But it's not over 'til the fat lady sings. Ego pumpin', clit throbbin' and sweat drippin', the smell of pussy fills the room. I push my lover back against the pillows before she can come up for air. Tongue thrust deep in her throat. She won't admit it, but she loves when I take over. It's gotten so she fucks me in such a way that I can't wait for my turn and neither can she. Sliding down her hard but feminine body, I find my way to her warm, wet burrow. Legs parting as my tongue arrives. This buck wants to get sucked and so I ask her how badly. I know I'll pay for this later, but I can't help myself. I tease a little more preparing for the kill. It is a wonderful thing, being in control. Girl will do just about anything I say. But I too have waited for this moment. My tongue slides between the folds that have grown puffy and wet. The taste is that of desire and love, bittersweet. I hear her moan and my own genitalia flutters. I can't help but reach between my legs, my body moving to my lover's rhythm as my tongue sings her song.

At impulse a finger knocks on her door, gently massaging the opening. Liquid cream running down the tip, I gently push her open. The deeper I go, the more I feel a pulling sensation beckoning me to come in. I watch this boy melt in my hands, as the woman in her rises and falls. Two fingers sliding in and out slow and steady, going deeper with every call. My own heart racing at the sight and sound of her loving it, her body moving to meet each thrust. There is no greater moment than when you watch your lover succumb with such trust.

Girl looks dead to the world now. My face is all aglow. I climb on top of her to resusitate. Gently, I kiss her face and push back her hair. She opens her eyes as her arms come around to hold me closer. I can see her contentment with the passing pleasures. I see the love she feels for me. The fat lady sang a glorious tune tonight. She sang a song that still plays in my heart. I lie awake in the quiet night air, listening, remembering her song.

R I T A M O N T A N A

Covering the Grey

EVERYWHERE I GO, I'M LOOKING for a new lover. I'm at a workshop for "Parenting Your Adult Children." Halfway through the session, we are to pair up with another person for some one-on-one. Boldly, I head for Ellen. Her good looks and dry wit attract me. Could she be the one?

Ellen is my height. Her hair—conservative rather than dykey—is honey blonde. Looks like a rinse covering the grey. She, slender as I am, is a late-blooming lesbian with two sons in their thirties. Same as me. As we talk, I find out she is seventy, ten years older than me.

Her voice reminds me of a purring cat. I feel a tug in my sex. After the workshop, we set a date to get together later in the week. The idea of flirting and lovemaking when I'm sixty-four, seventy-five, eighty, ninety—who knows the limit?—excites me.

On a warm Saturday, she takes me to Central Park, shows me parts I've never seen. We come to a fountain which could be in Italy or France, sit on the basin's edge, watch children float boats, sticks, balls. I catch her gazing at me, her eyes of azure drinking me in. Could she want me, too?

The following Saturday we meet at Battery Park for a picnic. I slice tomatoes, dripping tiny yellowish seeds and red pulp onto our improvised stone table, add it to a plate with St. Andrea cheese, pale-yellow-creamy, oozing from its white skin as it softens in the sun, and runs into the velvet, yellow-green avocado crescents. Touching my hand like a feather, she says, "Would you spend the night with me?"

My heart skips. I say, "Yes, I want to." We go to her apartment at dusk. Honeysuckle scents the evening as we pass a community garden. Lightning bugs slip in and out of the chain-link fence, mingling with city lights.

Her apartment is tiny. A stove, fridge, and sink are squeezed into an alcove. I go into a bathroom so compact you can brush your teeth while sitting on the toilet. A shower stall—no tub. I resist my usual urge to open the medicine cabinet. I don't want to have preconceived ideas about her. I don't want to know what pills she uses, what items sit on the shelves.

When I return to the room, she hands me a silk kimono. "Here, put this on, make yourself comfortable. I'll be out in a minute. As she goes into the bathroom, I peel off my clothes, put on the robe. She returns wearing a robe, too, the colour of her eyes.

"You look beautiful," I say. Still, I am worried. What if her skin is wrinkled, ugly? What if I am turned off by her body, by sagging, empty breast sockets, flaky flesh?

"You are beautiful, too," she says. "Mind if I put on some music—k.d. lang or Lucy Blue Tremblay, maybe? It'll help me relax."

"Lucy. I love Lucy. She's great to dance to." My hands are sweaty and my mouth dry. I want her and I am so scared. What if I've made a terrible mistake? I don't want to hurt her or be hurt myself.

Ellen has pared her life down to the bare essentials and seems almost monastic. Being here reminds me of the nearness of death, but as I bring her close to me as we dance, her heat brings back desire. Our robes drop open, as we move to an interior rhythm. Her body surprises me.

Only the skin of her neck and hands give away her years—as if they alone have dealt with the hardship of living. Her neck skin seems loose, as if she has shrunk into herself to protect against harm. Her hands have raised purple veins, coarse cross-hatched skin, enlarged knuckles, finger joints that bulge with calcium deposits. Ellen's unpainted, ridged fingernails are cut short. Her body, the colour of an

Alberta peach, creamy, pale, edged with blue, lavender, pink, is like a young woman's—small breasts, firm, erect, stomach soft, slightly rounded. My cunt is wet.

We press into each other, naked skin to naked skin. I give tiny kisses on her forehead, eyes, lips, chin, neck, ears. I move down her body, kiss her breasts, stomach.

She stops me. "Go slow. I'm shy."

"Can I touch you with my hands?" I ask, trembling with anticipation.

"Yes, but slow—it's been a long time."

As my hand touches her hairless mound, she whispers, "I'm afraid."

"Don't be. We won't do anything we aren't ready to do," I say, trying to reassure her and myself, too. "Come." I lead her to the single bed pushed up against the wall in the far corner of her studio. "Let me give you a massage."

She slides out of her robe, lays on her stomach on the bed. I sit down beside her, also naked, and begin rubbing her shoulders, her wing bones, move my hands down her back, travel along her spine, press my fingers into her soft sides, caress the triangle of down at the top of her buttocks—do not touch their milky roundness or forbidden tuck. I move my hands back up her torso, up her neck, cradle her skull, feel her vulnerability.

She sighs, turns over, places my hands on her breasts, moans. She sprawls on her back, her body open. Moving from the top of her head and down, I kiss her all over again, taste her saltiness, inch by inch until I reach her vagina, dip deep into her secret place. Her vagina clutches my finger like a new born baby, sucks it, pulls me deeper.

I lay on top of her, no longer afraid she will break under my weight. My nose nuzzles her hair which smells like rosemary, sage, basil. We rock our locked bodies, swoon in one another's arms. We separate, pillow talk, fall asleep.

Weeping wakes me. "What's the matter?" I ask.

"I don't know why, but love-making makes me so sad."

I sit up. The city lights illuminate her wet face in the darkened room. She leans into my chest, clutches me. "Hold me. Don't let me go," she sobs.

I wrap my arms around her. Distant horns and a siren penetrate the room. The lace curtain on the studio's sole window billows against my arm. "What's going on?" I ask. "Did I do something wrong?"

"It's not you—it mostly has to do with men, but even Allison, my ex, did it. They just wanted orgasms without emotional involvement."

"Oh," I said. I hold her, feel her rage, like a feral animal, press against me. My heartbeat speeds and I pull away from her. "Tell me about Allison," I say, as I move to the edge of the bed, pull the sheet up over my breasts, but I don't really want to know. I am not ready for this intimacy.

"She wouldn't talk to me when I woke in the middle of the night, upset. 'Go back to sleep,' she'd say, 'you'll be better in the morning.' But I wouldn't. I would remember how men used me, how mean my ex-husband was and my mother—how they all hated me."

Sadness wells up in me. I, too, want to tell her to go back to sleep. Comforting her feels too hard. The dark recedes as the sun begins to rise. "I've got to go," I say, as I get out of bed, put on my clothes. I lean over, kiss her pale lips, then head for the door. Looking back, I see Ellen staring at the ceiling, where she, too, must see the sliver of sunlight, in a rainbow prism.

EMILY GEORGE

Essential Connections

JAYNE EXPLORES THE MAP of her lover's body in order to work out where she is, where she's going, and what she's supposed to do along the way. Her fingers move lightly over the familiar contours of the female curves, noting the smoothness of skin, the softness of flesh, the shape of bone and muscle, so like and yet unlike her own.

Running her palm over the new thick crop of hair outlining her beloved's head, she is reminded of how it felt just a few short months ago, when it was so sparse and fine from the chemotherapy, Freda had taken to wearing a beanie to bed to keep warm.

Her heart still jolts at the sight of Freda's face smiling at her across a crowded room, even after these many years down the relationship track together; this dearly loved face with the whiskers curling out of the double folds of chin. The bulk of shoulders and upper arms, theatrical techie that she is, strong and capable of doing a multitude of skills, including being a base for the circus balances as a way of expressing her pride in herself and her body.

And these breasts that have never suckled any baby can, nevertheless, provide as much sustenance as any dyke might need. Jayne's mouth closes around the nipple as it hardens deliciously against her tongue, while her fingers circle the other nipple, hand fondling breast, burying her face in fullness, breathing in lesbian smell.

This white expanse of stomach, scarred now, not with stretch marks such as she'd seen on previous lovers. These slight puckerings of skin, almost faded, indicate the points of entry to remove the recalcitrant stone and gall bladder, hardly significant at all in the scheme of things.

Whereas, and here she traces down the long line of the radical hysterectomy scar from the navel to the pubic bone, this one defines such a momentous, terrifying, life-threatening and catastrophic time in both of their lives that just to recall it is enough to make her not want to have to go through the threat of cancer ever again.

And yet like most crises, this one had prompted changes that were long overdue in her life, so in that sense she had to be grateful for the opportunity to learn and grow and move onto other things.

"Your hair is definitely growing back," she murmurs, pulling lightly on the not so curly tufts that spring from the chubby mound of Freda's cunt.

"Thank goodness for that," Freda states with feeling. She'd been much more horrified by the complete loss of her pubic and underarm hair than by the near baldness of her scalp because, as she saw it, this secondary hair was symbolic of her adult womanhood and she hadn't liked losing it one bit.

"I look like a girl again," Freda would mutter in embarrassment when Jayne would say how beautiful the newly exposed folds looked in the palm of her hand. And nothing she said either comforted or dissuaded Freda from her grief and humiliation.

Jayne's middle finger makes a path through the springy hair into the crack where the pink labia lies hidden and finding the clitoris, moves ever so slowly and gently into the erogenous zone of ragged breath and trembling thighs.

Jayne has always marvelled at how different each orgasm is for every woman, the methods used, the intensity gained, the time it takes to reach the pinnacle before plummeting over the edge.

Freda squeezes her legs together and Jayne's hand stays absolutely still from the precise onset of orgasm onward. For herself, once the climax has started, she has to have the exact same movement on precisely the same spot all the way though to the end, all with her legs spread wide apart.

While she agrees, theoretically, that achieving orgasm is not the be-all and end-all, as she lies in the sweet aftermath of both their most recent achievements, she knows there's nothing else that comes even close to this kind of immense satisfaction.

She peers downward at her lover's legs spread-eagled in satiated relaxation, those muscled thighs that hold the weight of other women during circus pyramids, the knees scarred from childhood, the hairy calves, the dainty little feet with the plump toes.

"I love your beautiful little feet," Jayne murmurs and touches them with her own.

"I love you too, my darling," Freda moves toward her and without opening her eyes, Jayne turns her face up to be kissed.

Life is simply this, Jayne thinks; loving warmth, skin touching, solid connection, and her tongue exploring the inside of Freda's delicious mouth.

LYDIA KWA

This Place Called Absence

THE SUN APPEARS THEN DISAPPEARS behind clouds. The path through the park is full of people. We are pulses of the snake's body, throbbing with its life. Francis and I hold hands. Twinges of panic pass through me, electrical bursts rattling the gut. Morbid images of women and men with their bodies bleeding, bruised, or marked by hate, flash through my mind. Daylight might not protect us from attack. I turn away from observing people, and look at the ocean instead. I keep on holding her hand, even though part of me feels like fleeing.

How surreal it is to be two women lovers in a crowd of strangers, walking, walking. A sea of legs moving to discordant rhythms. Two gay men pass us by. Later on, three dykes together. These, unlike the others, look at us with knowing smiles, unafraid to show their approval.

Ocean of many moods. Softly caresses pebbles, retreats, then rushes forward, threatening to reach over the edge of the wall and engulf us. Francis and I are quiet together while all around us, chatter drifts in and out of earshot. The longer we walk in silence, the calmer I become. Anxiety gradually drains out of me.

My eyes sweep upward and across the Lions. Sometimes I forget.

I keep expecting that flat landscape of my childhood. I think of the mountains as large, looming presences which block the horizon, and I often wonder about what I can't see. The mountains appear immovable and stoic. I say "appear," because vision could make us forget the past, that they weren't always there, having originated from the depths of the earth, thrusting through the surface as molten or granite batholiths. Even now, there might be invisible shifts occurring deep within them. And every earthquake that reaches this landscape, however minor or major, must somehow register within its forms. The faults, the fissures, all the fragmenting consequences.

The stretch of beach just before we reach English Bay is populated by rock sculptures. Like UFOs they've arrived and colonized this area. I remember reading about these sculptures in the *Vancouver Sun*. Some man who understands how to place rocks one on top of another such that they don't topple, but stay firmly tip-to-tip. The remarkable balance in nature. That man's hands must be guided by a special kind of sensing. What kind of passion compels him to do this?

At the foot of Denman, a crowd gathers around a juggler on his unicycle. Kids dart about furiously, jumping in excitement, and one fatally dislodges her chocolate ice-cream onto the front of her pink Osh-Kosh overalls. Francis and I eat hotdogs and drink pop. We kiss. No one seems to notice.

We turn around and walk the same route back. Smell the sea.

The hours go by, unconsidered and irrelevant.

Back at her apartment, we undress each other to the languorous, rhythmic drip of the kitchen tap. One button, another, then another. Peeling away time and hesitation. The unhurried conversation of gestures. The needs of the skin, to remember how to welcome a stranger's touch, to shed resistance. Her crimson bra strap releases quietly in my hands. My hands are poised to extract truths; they cradle the weight of her breasts.

"Your hands are very warm," she whispers in my ear.

The weight of sheer breath. Laden, audible. *Quand elle me prend dans ses bras*. The whisper, *elle me parle tout bas*. Long kiss of tongue diving for depth. Her bare, vulnerable neck, as the throat opens. Primal emotions buried in the muscles of the voice.

I hold up her left hand to my nose. Smells of coffee, hot dogs, and ketchup. Soap and tobacco, and the complex questions of the body.

The mind's thought in the palm of her hand. I lick the lines: heart, head, life, health. The coded details of her fate.

I trace the origins pooled in her wrist, supple, complicated, continue the passage of longing up her arm, following the instinct of movement. My mouth grazes the mole over her heart. A dragon descends from the sky, fixing its fiery intent on her sacred mound.

With my hand, I part her. Separate surface from depth. Where the thighs meet. Where the rivers of the body's longing culminate. Sentiments, sediments. To taste her dense salt-drenched delta, and open her particular history with speech. The question of how, again and again. The sweat of seeking. *Alors je sens en moi, mon coeur qui bat*. I strain to reach the heart of her. Taut and wet presence.

She draws me up, her breathing close to my ear. I feel the sweat at the back of her neck, gracing the edges of her forehead. Her fingers reach down to that vulnerable place at the base of my spine. Her touch sets off a spreading ache, upturning my body from within, earth when air enters it, solid becoming less solid. Pausing above me, her breasts hovering, she's asking for surrender. Here where the soft vulnerable indentation is, where throat meets clavicle. She moves so that her hair sweeps across my chest. Small ripples awaken skin, cause whispers at the edge of a dark pool. Her hand dives into me, the echoes of her entry travelling deeper into my universe. Thinking with her hand, her mind in my body, her body in my mind.

A single swirling ache. Everything is rushing at me, through me. I fall in, merging with the current.

L. K. BARNETT

Private Rituals

NELLA LEANED BACK IN HER ROCKING CHAIR as she wiped sweat from her brow with the back of her wrinkled black hand. The old porch squeaked each time she rocked forward. Nella watched two light-skinned boys kick a tin can back and forth between them in the middle of the road and wondered how late in the day it was getting to be.

Muriel, Nella's friend, sat on the same porch in a relatively new wicker chair with bright floral pillows neatly placed behind her small back. Muriel looked at her watch and told herself it would soon be time to wash and snap the green beans and set the fat-meat to boiling for her and Nella's supper.

Muriel's long wavy hair fell loosely on her shoulders beneath a wide-brimmed straw hat. Her reddish-brown skin—Nella sometimes called her "Nutmeg"—was shining from the olive oil she religiously rubbed on her face to decrease her chances of getting too many wrinkles.

Nella's short coarse hair was parted down the centre. Two separate plaits started at the front of her forehead and ended by her ears. Tiny, tight grey curls, too short to braid, outlined her taut black face. She wore no hat. Both women were old. Both women had been young once and in love with each other. Their youth had escaped them—their love had not.

Nella often thought about the future, aging, while Muriel reminisced about the good ol' days—dancing to jazz music and Friday night fish fries with Jimmie and Gradie, those exquisitely dressed and extremely debonair sissies that'd looked out for she and Nella when they'd first come to Alabama. Thinking and reminiscing was their daily ritual.

Nella always found something "young" to stare at while she thought about growing old; usually it was an inanimate object, like a blooming flower. Today it was the two young boys who were kicking a noisy tin can between the two of them in the middle of the road.

Muriel fixed her eyes on Nella and smiled. I hope you want green beans, corn bread, and fat-meat tonight—'cuz that's what I'm in the mood for, Muriel thought; although the menu was subject to change if Muriel doubted for a second Nella wouldn't be pleased with it. Over the years Muriel and Nella had fed each other everything—comfort, home-made biscuits and gooseberry jam, passionate lips, understanding, collard greens, eager fingers, encouragement, ripe plums and green bananas, slippery tongues, advice, rich tapioca pudding, and love.

Muriel delighted in her daily ritual of preparing meals for the two of them. Nella enjoyed eating whatever Muriel prepared.

The young boys stopped kicking the noisy tin can when they heard a woman's voice call out, "Time to eat." Nella glanced over at her lover of forty-seven years and thought green beans, corn bread, and fat-meat sounded jes' fine, jes' fine.

The two smiled at each other in silent appreciation of their rituals.

RUSSEL BASKIN

Kissing Away the Memories

PHOTOS OF YOU STARE AT ME from across the room, evidence of the woman who still treads inside you. Visible rarely. Missed often. From my bed I watch you pull the rings off your hands, a part of your body which hasn't changed. You turn to look at me while you unbuckle your belt, unbutton your pants, slowly removing them from narrow hips, which have shed the soft fatty tissue, as you now shed your jeans, letting them slide to the floor in a heap. Your skin, darker than mine, is wrapped around defined muscles, displaying tension as you cautiously lift your t-shirt above your head. Naked underneath. My throat catches. Your scars barely visible, a reminder you were not always this way.

Your mound of dark curly hair now grows in masculine directions, but what lies underneath remains untouched by hands other than mine. I go there often to your beginning, to remember and pay homage to the past. A past which has me trapped, bound by love to the woman hovering under your surface. My feelings for you rage through my body, conflicting emotions pushing and pulling from head to heart to cunt. Relief comes when the wetness begins to flow between my legs as you move nearer, your brown eyes never leaving mine. How brave you are standing there, a warrior searching for my desire, undefended, camouflage removed as you strap on your leather harness like a missing birthright.

You lie close by my side.

We are separated only by the changes I want to erase with my caresses. Gently, I touch the contours of your chest, kissing away the memories in my mind. You bring your hand to my face. Your fingers trace the fullness of my lips and disappear into the warmth of my mouth, to the delight of my tongue. If I close my eyes, I can pretend nothing is different. Forget. Sometimes I want to forget.

Your tongue enters where your hand was and I match your need with my desire, demanding, urgent, as if this were our last time together. I try not to retreat from your recently shaved face, brushing across my skin like tiny needles.

You sense my distance, pull your mouth away, try to read me with your eyes.

"Don't stop," I say. "No words. Not now."

I take your hand, move it to my breast so you can feel my nipple harden, rising to your touch, and we swim back to a place between reality and dream. A moan escapes my throat. You smile.

"See, nothing has altered," you say.

Your tongue circles the outside of my nipple, teasing, then sucking. My hips move autonomously as I sway between the known and unknown territory of your body. I stray down your back, stroking the familiar bumps of each vertebra, covered by the smoothness of your skin, accepting the transition to leather, as I arrive at your harness gripping tightly, wishing I could make time stand still. You run your hand across my belly, damp with sweat, stopping to tease the ring in my navel, then letting your fingers travel through the thick curls of my pubic hair, before sliding them over to my clit, only to return again and again. My desire overrides your gender. All I want is to draw you deep inside me. You lick me from your fingers. I kiss me from your lips, then pull you down between the softness of your thighs, guiding you into me, groaning as you, cool and slippery, fill me with pleasure. You whisper your loving in my ear as you press yourself against me, thrusting into me. I match your hunger with my own. You are desperate, determined to hold us together, though we are being pulled apart by the same force which plunges your hips into mine, faster and harder, until my body bursts and my heart aches with longing for you, the woman, knowing I am hurting you, the man.

D I A N N E   W H E L A N

Her Hands

HER HANDS. THE FIRST TIME HER PALM wrapped itself around mine, I was humbled by size and moved by tenderness. We were walking through a busy bar. She reached back and took my hand into hers, as if to protect me. Her large hand, a warm blanket, her acknowledgement, a smile. It was a simple gesture that could have meant nothing but did mean everything. Passion thrives in simplicity.

When her fingers break open garlic, all the little cloves fall onto the cutting board like obedient children, bottoms up. The chopping looks like a casino dealer counting out a full deck. Fast, confident.

She likes using her hands. She knows they have power. Her hugs could make a boxer cry. That perfect balance between strength and tenderness. It's not just the size of her hands and fingers, it is the control and agility. Her passion is music. When she plays her guitar, her fingers dance. They are melody, beat and rhythm. She closes her eyes when she sings. I wonder where she goes to find the emotion she puts into her music. If I closely watch her hands, they will take me there. For I know they are with her.

When we make love, she surrenders before she takes. It is then that my small hands take hers and she gives them to me. I place them down to the sides of her head on the pillow and my fingers worship her palms as my mouth slides over her mouth to her nipples, her belly, her thighs. It is then her hands quiver and grip mine.

Her hands have healed, they have built, they have held, and they have fucked. I have had her fingers so deep inside me, they unleash dreams. I have awakened on the crest of a large sand dune, amidst a sea of dry waves. I watch a black raven circle overhead, casting an enlarged shadow on the sand's surface. In the distance, the mountains shimmer, the air fluid movement. In my hand, one cold bottle of water, precious blood in this dry land. When I go to drink, it is her mouth I awaken to and her hands I feel surfing the contours of my body. It is her hands that take me there. It is her hands that bring me back. Her hands make me want to give it all to her, every last outpost of my thoughts, every salty tear of my fears. It is her hand I want to hold through glory and despair, through birth and death. Her hands. Always, it is her hands.

RITA WONG

Touch: A Natural History

I CONSTANTLY TOUCH MY HAIR, smooth it down, feel it silky against my fingers in a moment's catch, attached to its sensations, how heat soaks into it, how it defends against cold, how it brushes against my cheeks and nose and flies bravely in the wind. my fingers feel the cool smoothness of skin, of legs, of flannel warmth in a soft bed, rough denim in the morning, dressing rituals, reassuring cotton on my aroused body, towel damp, drips of bathwater slip off skin. i know my world through touch, my world is my body. i know its rough skin, smooth skin, scratchy hair, silky hair, like my tongue knows its home—the mouth, its cohorts the lips. my toes dig into soft carpet, my ankles know rough wool, fingers feel the cold table and the solid fork, the firmness of chopsticks, utensils part of food. the slide of water against itchy skin. the loop of sensations the fingers absorb, tap the rhythm of a slow morning ease into feeding at noon. the paper rub of books as pages flip, pen in hand, the comfort of bodies, the comfort of food. always, touch fills the arms, surges into the breasts and down my hips. touch i am full of her. touch is warm is real is familiar yet surprising a forest of hair. i am touched cold finger to warm head, wet fingers to warm thighs. touch is the determination to feel the world on fingertips, each grain of sand has a trail tongue on skin, on soup, on rice. skin against a cold nose. touch knows if someone is too close or not close enough, rubbing against invisible fences.

D O N N A   A L L E G R A

On Scent as Memory's Keepsake

I CURL FINGERS UNDER MY NOSE and relish my aroma. Nothing in the world smells like pussy. The scent contains the musk of a gym locker room, a hint of baking bread and the salt of human flesh stitched in.

Such a basic, universal scent. The variation in pussy vapors that interests me most is its magnitude in a woman—lightly steamed or cooked heavily in juices. My favourite fragrance is the menstrual brand.

Alongside the pussy breath taking me to sex's bed, my nose trails a woollen blanket smell—the locker room again—clothing bunched up, damp with sweat. Scent serves as memory's souvenir from a time when I dreamed of being the gym teacher I am now.

But once upon a time I was a high school kid with Karen. As I press closed an open gym locker, I recall the first time we had sex. I wasn't sure then it *was* sex.

Eighth-period gym class. No one else was around. The fingers of Karen's left hand had palmed my pubis and I spread my legs further to give her room. She lets her hand caress the triangle at my lap and my hips circle in response to her finger's inquiry.

I hum from my throat to keep her feeling me up. Her hand massages the valley between my legs. A door of pleasure opens inside. This place has existed underground, but comes magically to life with her abracadabra of touch.

I pump, inviting her hand to push further. I want her to voyage within the cave of flesh and space. This is an area my own fingers do not ordinarily explore. When I hike the trail of sexual feeling I blaze for myself, the heart of my palm remains outside my body as it strokes against my pubic mound. Karen's fingers don't quite enter the threshold of my body's house. Still, they shake the windows that rattle me, unlocked in my own home.

I want her hand whistling within where I'm gushy with feeling and heat. I've become the consistency of tapioca pudding. I melt like Quaker oats made thick, the water boiled off, when her long finger finally slides into me.

My clit lolls outside my labia like a dog's tongue. It dribbles a white spittle from the pudding my inner organs have stirred to. All my body insists its attention to the delta between my legs. My entire being declares this valley of life-feeling-like-death-entering-ecstasy is the only important place.

"Ummmmm," I mewl, the sound of my voice applause for her hand clasping me as I buck and circle my haunches.

I can feel Karen smiling into my neck. Her right arm cradles my back. "Easy, baby," she says as she humps my thigh with a mild pulsing, her hand grazing casually. The fulcrum of her strength powers her left hand and her trivet of fingers plays me.

Somehow this stroking feels more piercing through the fabric of my white cotton gym shorts. I exhale like a tea kettle, whistling urgently from a nozzle that allows only a thin stream to release.

I don't know if this desperate sweetness is love or sexual perversion or what. I only know I don't want her to stop feeling me up. We'd been eyeing each other for months: circling around in gym class, drawing near in the hallways between periods, sniffing each other out in Mrs. Reis' honours English. I'd catch her staring and she'd see my eyes dart away. This is what we've both been wanting, though I couldn't have said so or even known before we touched like this.

The scent of my sex cooking under her kneading hands is the smell of her success. It mingles with the sweaty flesh of her forehead at my neck, as she hunkers against my loins.

I decide I won't ever ask Karen what perfume she wears. I want it to remain unknown. It can be one more piece of mystery about her. Even if I could go out and buy the scent for myself, it's her body chemistry at the base of it which holds the magic.

She slows her stroke from an arpeggio to a strum. I'm not willing to give up the stronger rhythm my body exudes. I'm still strung tight, but she's strumming me like a Stradivarius.

I fight not to moan, yearn to bellow for her to complete my pleasure. I feel distressed but dare not make plain that I crave more touch, that she make a steeper climb at my Mount of Venus. I was just going to let her feel me up a little and look where we are. My fever isn't over yet, but I let myself subside.

And just as well. We startle when footsteps echo down the hallway, heading toward our gym lockers. I want to shriek like a referee's whistle for the person to stop and go back. We break apart from each other, pretending nothing has happened between us that should not. Our faces compose ready lies in case whoever walks that corridor arrives at our lockers. We are just two girls getting dressed to leave after gym and go to our next class, almost ready to depart.

❦

I let memory slip from the scent of my fingers. It was a lifetime ago that I was a teenager having sex after gym. I walk slowly past several lockers, purposely making my footfalls loud. I close a locker door that would block an oncoming person's view and I come to a halt.

"Everything okay, girls?" I ask, careful not to look too closely at Keisha and Lamar. The pair seem decidedly casual about getting dressed after our team practice.

"Yes, fine, Ms. Marks."

"See you at tomorrow's game then."

I raise a hand from the clipboard and place my thumb on my chin, fingers under my nose as if I'm about to utter something more, but think better of it. I inhale and don't say a word. I smile briefly at the faces that don't look up to my eyes with their usual eagerness and I leave the two girls alone.

SPIKE HARRIS

Your Alley

TODAY IS YOUR BIRTHDAY. Tomorrow is mine. If you were alive, you'd be forty-four.

I dropped my current squeeze off at your building today. Your friends had left balloons floating in the courtyard in honour of your birthday. One of them caught me, wrapped itself around my neck.

Your friends are sweet to me, but they keep our secret quiet. I am on the periphery, outside of what is being done in your honour. We agreed at the time to keep our affair secret. It would have been too complicated to have people know, because we worked together. I'm touched when your friend who still lives in the building makes a point of talking to me about you, of when you went camping together, and how your daughter is.

If you were alive today, maybe today would pass with only a phone call to wish you a happy birthday. Maybe you'd get your happy birthdays in for me in the same call. Or maybe we wouldn't talk at all. Our whole relationship was unpredictable. I hadn't seen it coming.

I was leaving your house one night, after dinner and drinks. I really thought I was going home. It was late, you walked me to the door, and everything felt different. I could tell you wanted me to kiss you.

And you certainly weren't surprised when I asked. I knew I shouldn't do it. I knew our lives could become a mess if I followed you up those stairs. The whole idea was forbidden, but leaning down into you, kissing you, felt so warm and right. Everything about you was inviting and enticing and dangerous.

I followed you to your room. We kissed again, my hands around your waist, taking in the feel of your body, savouring it like something sweet on my tongue. We fed on each other that night until the sun came up. I heard the birds singing outside as I fell asleep.

When I woke up, you were standing above me, handing me a cup of coffee and offering me a shower. You were already dressed. You were talking to your daughter, who was brushing her teeth in the bathroom. And then you left, went to the corner to catch your ride to work. "See you there," you said, as the door closed behind you.

Over the course of that summer, a lot of mornings started that way. You would leave, go to the corner, and get your ride to work. I would wander into the office after you, and when we saw each other, we would act as if we were bumping into each other for the first time that day. If everyone wandered away, we would take a minute to check in, and then go back to the act of being normal co-workers. Usually, when the day was over we would go home to our own places. Sometimes I would get a call from you, and it would all begin again.

Then one day it stopped. I never knew why, it just didn't happen again.

To know I was losing you, to know you were dying, and to have had an affair we never told anyone about was like holding a molten rod in my hands and not crying out. When everyone was crying over losing you, it didn't seem the right time to tell them we had been lovers, though I confess I had moments when I wanted to scream it. The secrecy continues today. I sit at home and think about the nights we spent on your balcony, laughing and talking and how each time I thought it was time to go home, I didn't.

When I look back on my life, I see points where I was in a river, drifting, being pulled down into a tributary. I guess that's what happened to us. One day the current shifted and the water started running to new places. We were carried downstream in different directions.

I always drive by your alley on my way home from work, and I throw you a little wave. The alley was an artery that ran between us. I still think of you, see it as a part of you, each time I pass it. Some nights I retrace my steps, taking myself right past the place we used to sit. Right up to and then past your door.

I live in silence. About you. About me. We were two halves of a secret, and now I just have my half. It's something I can hold in my hand, but can't describe to anyone else. When I try to talk, the words are like stones I am trying to skip across a lake, bouncing from point to point. They only touch the surface, never sink down into the truth.

I guess I'm no longer afraid about people finding out about us. I no longer think it's the worst thing that could happen.

M A U R E E N   K I N G

Untarnished Love

MYFANWY MORGAN ARRIVED HOME. It was an effort to bar the door, for the wind was giving no respite. She picked up an old woven shawl, threw it over her bent shoulders, and proceeded to jam some sticks and twigs into the old stove that leaned precariously against the bellying wall. She put a blackened kettle onto the stove and sat down at the littered wooden table—rocking its swollen legs against the uneven flagstones to reach for a chipped mug. She picked up a loaf of bread and started to cut away, but the knife she'd used was almost not there—its blade was so thin halfway down, it shuddered and vibrated like a musical saw under her hungry assault. She tried to spread the hard butter but only succeeded in tearing the loaf. She resorted to slicing the butter finely, sticking it flat against the bread.

Myfanwy gulped her strong, sweetened tea with relish—she loved to swallow the tea-leaves. Not for her those awful teabags people use today. She chomped through her bread and butter with such violence, it made her false teeth click like knitting needles. She wiped the butter off her mouth with the back off her hand. After filling her needs, she stood up and reached for her pipe that lay on the old three-legged dresser—the missing leg replaced by several thick slates.

The stove was beginning to warm the room in spite of the wind's interference, and Myfanwy relaxed a little. Peering around the room she thought, not a lot really, after all those years of slaving, not much to look at. As she slowly looked around, the pipe smoke followed in abeyance in short, quick, bursts. She'd had enough of her pipe and put it back in its usual place, and tried to stretch herself by pulling her shoulders back as far as they would permit. "Mustn't sit around too long," she muttered, "otherwise I'll rust up like the rest of the place."

Myfanwy hated going to bed. No lover to snuggle up to. No lover to tend her needs, no intimate touching, or familiar scent. Yes, she sighed, no one at all. It was never warm in her bedroom. She virtually undressed and dressed for sleep, wore bed-socks, and long-johns. On her upper body she had a large woolly cardigan, which had stretched over the years through too much washing and hanging. The only decent piece of furniture that had survived the passing years was the small round table her father had bought for her wedding. She looked at her wedding photograph by her bedside. John, her late husband, was sitting down looking so full of himself in his new britches and coat. That perky proud moustache of his, no matter how much he groomed it, stuck out at a slight angle, giving him a permanent quizzical expression.

It was beginning to get cold. Myfanwy snuggled into her cardigan and wondered how long before sweet sleep would overcome her. She would never forget her wedding day. What bitter thoughts had gone around in her mind that day. Dear John never knew, thank God. She had never loved John, or shall we say, was never in love with him. But she did grow to love him—love without passion or mystery.

She'd only been sixteen at the time. It was summer, and the whole countryside was bursting at the seams with warmth and friendliness. She loved everyone that summer, but only fell in love once.

Sweet, sweet Mary, Myfanwy thought, how I've longed for you all these years. She remembered when they had first kissed in the cow shed. The thrill of that taboo kiss had overflowed into a singing stream. They had been like innocent children and felt no wrong. The purity of their love made them incautious, and because of their innocence, they didn't think to hide behind subterfuge. They'd roam the woods and lay in the sweet, green grass, holding hands, kissing with a hunger that surprised them both. They carved their love on their favourite tree, in their secret place. But their innocence was their undoing. Ignorant-minded folks began to whisper foul thoughts. Myfanwy's mother caught them lying naked in their secret place, and the whole world became obscene and profane. No matter what her mother screamed, Myfanwy could never accept that their love had been corrupt. She never saw sweet Mary ever again.

"Time you got married, my girl," her mother had said repeatedly. Feelings of dread spread through Myfanwy like water in a sponge. She compromised and married John. He had been a good patient man. Hadn't minded coming to live on Myfanwy's family farm. Yes, she thought, he had worked hard, for too long. The wind always won in the end. The soil had been eroded by the cruel, ceaseless winds, wiping all before it, like shifting sands, leaving hardly anything growing.

Myfanwy was beginning to get drowsy, and wished with all her heart she was lying next to her dear Mary. Even to this day Myfanwy could smell Mary's special scent. It had always reminded her of daisies, and fresh hay. Perhaps it was because they used to play "Love me, love me not" with the daisies, pulling out the petals one by one, until one of them declared that she loved the other more. Myfanwy remembered swearing that she'd love Mary forever and ever, and as it happened, it turned out to be true. She was feeling wonderfully tired now, floating. It wasn't cold anymore, and she couldn't feel her aches and pains. Even the normally impenitent wind was whispering gently in its sleep.

S H A N I   M O O T O O

Lemon Scent

HER PALE BROWN HANDS, skin fine and smooth like brushed silk, clutch an oval silver tray against her yellow sari in the area of her navel, indenting lightly. I look down at her offering—faintly wrinkled, reddish black prunes. Careful not to linger to contemplate the shape of the hands, the impeccably manicured shiny-shell-pink fingernails, I concentrate, instead, on spaces between the score of healthy-looking prunes slit slightly and stuffed plump with peanut butter, the slits sealed over with firm pink icing. The spaces between the prunes reveal a white, linen-textured paper doily embossed with low relief paisleys.

The outer edge of her oval tray brushes against the area of my navel. Above the tray there is a heat growing, filling the space between her and me, and the smell of her cologne on fire thickens to fill up the space. I trace paisleys in the spaces between the prunes with my eyes.

I am careful not to imagine the warm smell of her skin, behind her ears, on the back of her neck. Grasping the tray tightly with her right hand, she obscures my paisleys with her left, fills my view with her hand. Between thumb and middle finger she picks up a prune. Her forefinger guides it from behind up toward my mouth.

I am careful not to look into her eyes.

A little shaft of light glimmers off the band of her gold wedding ring as it catches the light from another room. As her hand reaches my mouth I look over her shoulder to the other room. Her husband stands leaning against a wall sipping his drink, chatting with his friends. I barely open my mouth and her cologne rushes against the back of my throat. Her fingers touch my lips. My tongue flits against her forefinger. The heat and smell of her cologne, like a pounding surf, fill up my mind.

I am careful not to linger.

ꝺ

He looks out the kitchen window with the phone pressed to his ear. Down the hill from that side of his house run miles and miles of undeveloped forested land—wild samaan, giant ferns, ginger lilies, bird-of-paradise bushes and palm trees, all meshed in suffocating philodendron vines—meeting the sea in the distance.

He doesn't really see what he is staring at. Level with his eyes is the horizon line where the faint sliver of white sea butts against the white sky.

His voice is distant, fading in and out of the bad telephone connection. His edges are softened with a gesture of deep concern.

" . . . has everything she could ever want but . . . I don't understand . . . is sulking, her depression again, you know . . . I am going out for some drinks with the guys from work tonight, so please come over. Spend the evening with her . . . I'll be back late, very late. Spend the night. Lately she only ever laughs when she is with you . . . I can count on you, can't I . . . ? I don't want her to be unhappy. . . ."

He pauses, breathing in faint traces of his wife's lemon-scented cologne that lingers around the mouthpiece of the phone. Reaching across meandering miles of rough country roads, the line's crackling ceases long enough for him to utter a scared, masked warning: "I must not lose her."

He hangs up the telephone, shoves his cold hands into the back pockets of his blue jeans, and absently looks out the window across the rolling green lawn, dotted here and there with lone hibiscus and croton that his wife conscientiously tends, to the wire and concrete fence that surrounds his property.

He stops at the door of their bedroom before entering and anxiously watches her, his prized exquisite accomplishment, envy of his men friends, huddled in a lifeless puddle on the bed. Standing in the doorway he is not fully at ease informing her that soon he will be leaving and that he has invited Anita over to keep her company for the evening.

An image of Anita and his wife talking intently and at length, almost shyly, at a party recently, comes to his mind. She seems to sizzle with life in Anita's presence. He hopes that his gesture will charm her to him. He sees her chest flutter. Her breathing quickens noticeably.

She uncurls herself and slowly emerges from the bed. He walks over to her and reaches hopefully for her waist, but she glides in and out of his fingers before he can pull her towards him. Knots of fear are beginning to cramp his stomach. Gradually his eyes harden, redden with anger.

Sitting on the edge of the bed, pulling on heavy grey-and-red sports socks, twisting and shoving his feet into greying leather running shoes, he glances up at her every few seconds.

At her dresser she stands leaning in toward the mirror, brushing her long, wavy black hair until it fluffs out light and full around her face and down her back. He has the impression that she is brushing out her hair more thoroughly than usual. He watches her in the mirror, hoping that she will look over at his pleading face. Without taking her eyes away from her face in the mirror, she offers him a cup of tea before he leaves, but he can feel that her intention to make it is weak and unwilling.

From his stillness in the room, she knows that he is watching her as she readies herself for Anita's visit. Nervously she rambles, saying that if it rains the eaves on the roof will overflow because they need to be cleared of the leaves shedding from the poui tree in the backyard. He does not answer.

He watches her shake the bottle of lemon cologne into her hand. She rubs both hands together lightly, quickly dabs behind her ears and pats her neck, running her hands down onto her chest, the palms brushing her breasts. She pours more cologne into her hand and rubs it on the small mound of her stomach, massaging it. When she turns to walk over to her closet he gets up and crosses over to the dresser to brush his hair. Looking straight into the mirror at his own reflection, he says more loudly than is necessary, "I'm really glad that you have such a good friend in Anita."

She pulls a dress so forcefully off its hanger that the hanger springs away, snapping off the metal rod and clanging to the wooden floor. He continues, "I wonder why she isn't yet married. She is a bit of a tomboy . . . not exactly appealing to a man. Do you think she is attractive?"

With her face still facing the open closet, she manages to pull up the zipper on the back of her dress by herself. He walks over to her and puts his hands on her waist. He turns her around and cups her face with his hand. With half a grin, as if cautioning her, he adds, "You know, she might be one of those types who likes only women."

He drops one hand to his side and with the other he grabs her face along her thin sharp jaw line and pulls it up to his. Uncured sharp lemon scent settles bitterly on the back of his tongue. With his lips almost against hers he whispers, "If I ever find out that you two have slept together I will kill you both."

He presses his opened mouth onto hers, pulling her lower lip into his mouth briefly. He smoothes back the hair from her face, turns and leaves.

MARIA V. MANDULOVA

That is All I Have from Yuly

"RELAX," SAID MONIKA IN HER DEEP VOICE as we climbed the stairs. "He's more effeminate than we are."

"I guess so," I said, my eyes measuring the bulky muscles of her trained arms. She gave me a smile and rang the bell. The transy opened the door. Indeed, he wasn't much of a man. He was more beautiful than I had imagined. He had long dark wavy hair and piercing green eyes. It was obvious that he didn't shave his face, for it was perfectly smooth. I would never have known he wasn't a real woman if I had met him on the street.

We entered the small apartment. It was cosy and neat. The transy shook my hand and said in a high-pitched voice, "I'm Yuly." His hand was thin and bony.

"I'm Anna. Glad to meet you."

"Have a seat, make yourself at home," he said.

There were drinks and cookies on the table. And a big vase full of chrysanthemums. He sat in an armchair opposite me.

"How long have you known each other?" I asked.

"We're old friends," Monika answered. "We met in the train to Sofia some five or six years ago."

"And right there on the spot I knew she was the one for me," Yuly smiled at Monika.

"I thought guys like you have boyfriends," I said.

"A common misbelief," Yuly laughed. "Well, not me. I have Monny; she's more than a boyfriend." He laughed again. "We have a wonderful time together. Would you like to join us?"

I hesitated. "I've never been through anything like that."

"You needn't worry about it," he said.

"I don't do it with men. I just can't."

"Can't you see I'm not quite a man? Don't you like me?"

"Give it a try," Monny said. "He doesn't behave as a man."

Yuly stood up and let loose his dressing gown. It fell onto his feet. His body was slender and very womanly although he had flat breasts and a small penis.

"Touch me," he said, "please, touch me."

I must admit he was attractive in spite of the male genitalia. I first caressed his thigh, then his stomach, and I rose to embrace him. He kissed my neck just below my ear and it gave me a thrill all over my back and my shoulders.

"I'll leave you alone for a while," said Monny.

I was suddenly embarrassed, but then I looked into Yuly's eyes and I knew he would never hurt me. We continued touching and kissing each other after Monny left the room. I didn't feel for him the passion I had felt for women, but his touch was nice and comforting.

"Isn't it a bit strange that you are attracted to girls?" I couldn't help being curious about Yuly's desires.

"Isn't it strange that you are attracted to girls?" he smiled back at me. "I've always wanted to be a woman. I adore the shapes of your bodies, the sound of your voices, the grace in your movements. I've suffered so much for not being one of your gender. And maybe God heard my prayers, or, as some psychotherapists believe, it was the result of my own suggestion, for my will was so strong that my brain affected my physiology and stopped the development of my male body. But God's will or my own, whatever it was, it couldn't transform me into a woman. So I'm saving money to go abroad where they perform transsexual surgery on people like me. I'm working hard for that's pretty expensive."

"What kind of work?"

"I paint greeting cards. I'm doing quite well. And they don't want me to show my passport to prove my identity when they pay me. That's good because with my passport it gets really embarrassing, for it says I'm a man and I don't look like it. People get shocked, and some are very aggressive."

"Have you got any friends?"

"Not many. The queer bird that I am, very few could stand my personality. Do you think you and I could make friends, Anna?"

"I don't know. Maybe." I had already begun to feel a tender affection for him. I couldn't be his lover, but I could be a friend. I didn't mind the tenderness we exchanged as we talked.

"Call me someday," he said, helping me with my coat. Monika was waiting for me at the front door. I gave Yuly the address of my landlady in Sofia, just in case.

"I'll call you, I promise. I'll see you very soon," I said.

But it never happened. The next day I left for my hometown to help my mother with the household. I stayed there for a week. When I was back in Sofia I dialled Yuly's phone number from the first phone booth I saw. Nobody answered. Some days passed and I kept calling three times a day, but Yuly didn't answer at all. Then I called my friend Monny to see if I had written a wrong number in my notebook. No, the number was all right, but something else was wrong. During my short absence Yuly had left the earth I was standing on. Some people had beaten him to death for being a homosexual.

"He wasn't even a homosexual." That was the first thing that came to my mind, and as soon as I said it I realized the total irrelevancy of these words at that moment. I went back to my lodging. The landlady had left my mail on the table. There was a small packet among the letters. I opened it: a full set of hand-made greeting cards for all holidays during the year.

That's all I have from Yuly.

MERCIA SCHOEMAN

The Healing

"MY MOTHER MUST HAVE HAD A PREMONITION," Zodwa often joked about the spontaneous intertwining of her name and her sexuality. Being the youngest of five daughters, her name means *only girls* in Zulu.

She grew up in a society where black women were sometimes raped by policemen shoving clubs up their insides until they were swollen and spongy. Afterward, a woman sometimes begged for water to rinse the blood and teeth from her mouth. A policeman, putting his boot on her throat until she started choking, guffawed that he would help her clean herself up and pissed in her mouth, then forced her head backward and aimed for her nostrils.

She could hardly remember her father, she told me, but she had an image of him as a strong man with hands like a tree, smelling of dark freshly ploughed soil after rain, almost as she imagined a black God would be. But the ANC was still banned under Vorster, God was not allowed to be black, and her father was detained during the 1976 riots.

The grey, however, she never forgot. Every memory of her youth seemed to present itself through pale layers of dust and smoke. Every morning, rising early to catch the train to school, the knobbly, pot-holed, dirt road stained her white socks with dust until she could grind it with her teeth. Usually the colourless sun was still struggling to free itself from the lingering mist, and dull orange candlelight occasionally seeped through door-casings and sackcloth curtains. The air smelled of sour milk and burnt plastic.

Occasionally she looked back over her shoulder at House 2587A, Zone 5, Meadowlands, Soweto, at the three wilted plants with dusky green leaves in empty Dulux paint tins in front of their house (to which her family kindly referred to as a garden) and wondered whether it would still be there when she returned in the afternoon.

Every day her mother's face was strong. The high-sickle-moon forehead and polished cheekbones seemed to be cautiously chiselled from rich ebony and her voice and body completed each other in perfect rhythm. But after she started dressing in a domestic servant's white uniform and *kopdoek*, her eyes could only follow her feet.

After school Zodwa used to play top-top, soccer, hide-and-seek, or housie in the rusty wreckage of an old car. Playing housie initially posed a dilemma for her, as she was not sure whether she wanted to be the mother or the father—or perhaps neither?—because during the same year of his arrest the authorities officially informed her mother that her father committed suicide in his cell.

They could not say how he did it.

I could listen to Zodwa for hours, learning about a history that I was part of and yet did not know at all, delving into the mysteries of a faintly familiar nightmare as if I had just woken up, feeling like a stranger under my light skin and wondering if she could ever heal enough wounds to love me.

"After they caught us playing housie one day, one of the older women took me inside, pulled down my pants and examined me. She wanted to see if I was of both genders, a man and woman—*isitabane*. Of course she could find no dick on me. . . ."

Later, when the ANC took its first breaths of freedom as a legal, political organization, some members declared that black people are not inclined to homosexuality, that it is an un-African import and a decadent white contamination of black culture. Some gangs in the black community took this to heart and appointed themselves lesbian bashers. And the *tsotsi* boys only knew one cure—the same as the police—fucking.

"Before we go any further, I must show you something," she said as she started to unbutton her shirt. I wanted to move closer, wanted to open her arms and taste her darkness, but as she pulled her shirt over her shoulder I could not move. The scar, when healing, shrunk her skin together in a bundle of white, knotty pieces of flesh, hanging like a ghostly full moon against the soft night of her skin.

"See, at least part of me knows how it feels to be white."

I was too embarrassed to touch her, too angry, perhaps too scared.

Her fingers unbuttoned my shirt, moving down to my jeans. The people swayed like a stormy sea, chanting *Amandla Awethu*, she lifted her fist and a nervous policeman started shooting. Four killed, an unknown number wounded. We've got her, the fuckin' faggot and her friends, the trouble-makers, said the one policeman as he kicked her into the back of the van. We are going to have some fun, boys, and the blood dripped down her legs, into her shoes.

She started rubbing my clit, round and round, harder and harder, until I felt my blood warming, thickening between my legs. I closed my eyes, felt how her one finger disappeared in me, pushing deeper and deeper into my body, later two, then three fingers. I groaned for more. She opened me like a wound . . . more, please, I want more of you. I want to open myself and suck your world inside mine. Her whole hand disappeared in my cunt, her fingers branching out in the thick fluids of my body. She clenched her fist, moving and kneading my insides, anchoring herself in me. This time no shots were fired . . . *Amandla Awethu* . . . her body was like soil and I was growing out of her, her mouth like a flower in my ear until my grip around her arm stiffened, again and again.

Long after she removed her hand, I could still feel her.

I noticed that her hand and arm were moist, covered with my thick white fluids and the smell of butter. She tasted her fingers, smiled as I softly started licking my way down to her scar.

---

kopdoek: Afrikaans for headscarf

isitabane: Zulu word for hermaphrodite. It is widely believed in the townships that homosexuals are hermaphrodites.

tsotsi: black gangster

Amandla Awethu: Power to the people

LORI SHWYDKY

Cherry Pie

SISTER MARIA FLOURED THE BOARD and pressed down expertly with the wooden rolling pin, the handles slightly worn, yet comfortable in her grip. The fat, white dough ran against the rolling wood, meekly rising for one last attempt at resistance before lying flattened. Her hands, their supple light skin so cherub-like they could have been kissed by the Virgin Mary herself, moved deftly over the dough creating an even, uniform crust. Her image of calm was flawless except for the deepening angry tracks that followed the edges of the pin on the pastry.

The hour was early, but the forest surrounding the church grounds reflected the cascading sunlight. The kitchen, dimly lit, polished and practical, cast an oversized shadow of Sister Maria that seemed to beckon toward the open doorway. A framed picture of Jesus, one hand held up, palm out, hung overhead. The room was quiet. Sister Maria ran cold water over her hands at the sink. From the window, steamed and sweaty from the kitchen heat, she could see Sister Teresa kneeling in the church garden, pulling weeds. The early summer crop of herbs and vegetables peeked timidly out from the rich, dark soil, but the weeds brazenly grew hearty and strong—they always did, she thought. In admiration she watched Sister Teresa deftly uproot the offending plants and carefully extricate each and every rootlet; much like the Divine Hand of Intervention, she mused, ready to save the Righteous Ones too meek and vulnerable to save themselves. She noticed the strong line of Sister Teresa's back against the loose grey t-shirt, and the fluffs of metamorphosed dandelions that rested momentarily on her hair before continuing their journey. All the while, Sister Maria's thumb inadvertently rubbed back and forth against the smooth curve on the edge of the rolling pin. Startled, her reverie was broken by the muffled sound of a deep, raspy cough. Father Ibex, she remembered, was working in the adjoining rectory stirring the biblical pages to set forth a brew of inspiration and admonitions for Sunday's sermon. She straightened her apron and moved away from the window.

Sister Maria lifted a can of cherry pie filling from the cupboard. The can rolled in her hand, the metal clinking against her ring. The gold band tightly encircled her third finger like a tourniquet, signifying her marriage to Jesus. She could no longer remove it.

Sister Maria was tired. She had been baking all morning in preparation for tomorrow's sale—the church needed still more renovations. She tipped the can and thick cherry filling spilled from the mouth of the container and settled slowly over the still-warm crust. An assortment of confectioneries surrounded her—her creations, all of them. Not once during the baking process had she raised a finger to her mouth to sample their sweetness. She lifted the remaining pastry layer and gently covered the exposed red filling. She stared at the concealed lumps of cherry that strained against the top crust. Somehow it brought to mind The Creation and she thought about Eve defying God and defiling man by eating of the fruit of the Tree of Knowledge. She tore off the over-hanging crust and fluted the edges. She was glad this pie was the last.

While the pie baked, Sister Maria cleaned meticulously to restore order. Her mind drifted to Sister Teresa and she pictured her long, slender, capable fingers plunged deep in the soil, hidden, but moving in easy fluid motion. She saw her face concentrated, her high, strong cheekbones smudged brown with a light film of dust brushed on by the back of a hand absentmindedly pushing aside stray strands of hair.

Cloth in hand, Sister Maria's knuckles whitened as she pressed down hard on the beige, speckled countertop. Her hand worked in furious, circular motion as she scrubbed at the bits of debris and cherry juice that tarnished the otherwise sparkling metal sink. She strived for a state of purity. "Cleanliness is next to Godliness," she reaffirmed to herself. On hands and knees, she clenched the sponge with both hands, sending a spray of soapy foam beneath the stove. She crushed the sponge against the baseboards as she scrubbed at minute particles of grime, visible to her eyes only. With steel wool that punished the sensitive, puffy, red skin around her fingernails, she relentlessly scoured all metal fixtures until each caught the lamp's image to reflect flashing points of light.

Sister Maria was the image of order and discipline, but her neat, polished black shoes dragged ever so lightly as she tread across the unblemished tiling toward the oven door. Drawn once more, she stopped at the kitchen window. Sister Teresa was still there, standing now, directing a slow, steady stream of water from the garden hose. Her hair, cropped short, curled wet at the ends against the nape of her neck. She raised the hose to her lips and drank. Sister Maria's fingers touched together, and her eyes, dilated in spite of the glare of the blaring noon sun, followed the flow of water as it ran past Sister Teresa's chin, down the front of her t-shirt, and downward still, creating streaks of clean white skin on her otherwise dirtied, well-muscled bare thighs. Just then, Sister Teresa looked up, spotted Sister Maria at the window, smiled, waved, and tipped the hose in greeting. Sister Maria's body stiffened, guilty like a voyeur exposed, and a sudden hue of crimson tinged her full cheeks. She bobbed her head in a quick nod, and half-raised her arm to return the wave, her motion unsure and jerky.

Quickly she moved away from the window, mindful of the mad pounding inside her chest, and reached for the oven door. The edge of the metal plate brushed against the tender skin between her thumb and forefinger as she set the pie atop the stove. She stopped and watched as a pinkness grew on her skin. Sounds of the pie filling erupted through tiny openings in the crust and fell back onto the stove. The red, gummy specks gleamed devilishly against the pure white of the oven and Sister Maria felt a stinging in her eyes. Water rose and tears spilled, mixing with the defiant specks of filling. A hard taste entered her mouth, like iron. She felt a heat take hold of her womb and rise like a fire in her belly, causing her stomach to clench with the pain of emptiness. Hunger consumed her. In an uncontrollable outburst of desire, she reached for the pie, plunged her smallest finger deep into the centre and sucked greedily. A low moan rolled in her throat, not rising. She looked in surprise at the thread of red glaze outlining her fingernail. Swiftly regaining her composure, Sister Maria washed her hands repeatedly with dish soap. Not once did she look toward the window. She placed the cherry pie amongst the other baked goods, the small hole in its centre creating a natural opening. She quickly recleaned the stove top.

Sister Maria bowed to the picture of Jesus hanging in the doorway and crossed herself as she left the room. Her hand reached back to switch off the light. Her polished black shoes moved in an orderly rhythm toward the prayer hall. Her feet dragged ever so lightly as she tread across the hard-wood floor.

RACHEL PEPPER

True to Nature

DIARY ENTRY, APRIL 18, 1990

My friend Justine tells me to wait, that I'm not ready yet. But all my life people have been telling me to wait, and I'm sick of waiting. I'd like to know how she's decided I'm not "ready." What the hell does she know?

Ever since she can remember, Una's been preparing for this moment. Lovers—first men, then women—have come and gone, and she herself has grown from a girl into a woman. It has always remained her one steady passion.

"One day, one day," she's always thought, when the mama urge rose up within her one like a rush of desire, uninvited but never unwelcome. It started when she was a teenager, with baby dreams coming to her intermittently in her sleep. As an adult, it's usually been a sharp pain, sometimes so strong in its poignancy it's made her cry.

Diary entry, August 17, 1996

There are so many babies at the Michigan festival this year that they've had to turn away kids from the child care area. Babies seem to be attached to every hip, breast, and back. I'm stunned to discover a girl I knew from early activism days in Chicago now has a newborn baby boy. I always thought I'd be the first of this generation of girls to have a baby and bring it to the festival with me. Now I see that this movement has happened without me at the forefront. It's a shock to realize that I'm now only following in someone else's footprints. This doesn't sit well with me. One more reason to get busy.

Where does this desire come from, she's often wondered. Is it innate? Somehow predetermined, stamped into her genetic passport like having hazel eyes and a big butt? Shaped by cultural forces like Baby Gap and swing sets? She doesn't care, she just knows it's her destiny. There has never been any doubt about that. But telling other people about it has always been harder.

Her friends uniformly have been skeptical, then eventually warily accepting of her urge to conceive. Telling her family was the worst. When she finally broke the news to her mother on the phone, it felt like a huge burden to shed.

The words "I'm starting to try to get pregnant" spill out like a confessional. She awaits the judgment, heart pounding.

"Do you think you need to have a child to feel complete?" her mother asks, after a moment's pause.

The words cut across Una like a cold dry wind. Under different circumstances, she knows, this question wouldn't be asked. If she were straight, if she were married, this desire for a child would be considered normal, a proper rite of passage. It's because she's queer, because she's single, the facts weigh differently in other people's brains.

Una's hurt but tries to spell it out for her mother as clearly as she can. She reminds her mother of the long-standing subscription to Parenting, the books on pregnancy and childbirth lining her bookshelves, the box of baby clothes in the closet, her stints as a camp counselor, substitute teacher in a local pre-school, and all the children she's developed friendships with over the years. She resists the urge to remind her mother of all the straight women who never wanted children, who've never even held a newborn until they have one.

"I'm different," she wants to scream. "My desire makes me different." Una wants to know how it is that with all the signs so blatant, she can still be so misunderstood.

The act of conception may only take a few moments or at most, a few hours, but actively planning a baby takes months. So many blood tests for diseases she's never heard of, so many choices of donors, so many fertility signs to check for. It's a whole new reperatory, a whole new vocabulary. She just wants a baby, but there's so much more to it than that.

Finally, the day nears for her first insemination attempt. She's speeding toward her most fertile moment, a speculum's been bought and sits primed, the cooler's packedwith dry ice and two vials of sperm from donor number 316. From the bathroom where the cooler sits, the eerie glow of potential life force reaches out to her in some secret, coded message all its own.

Diary entry, May 15, 1997

I'm so ready to start this. My body feels so lush. Like red velvet's wrapped itself around me. There's a humming under my skin. My body's announcing the inevitable to me.

It seems that after months of arranging and rearranging every last detail this moment would never come. There has been so much anticipation, and like the buildup to a long awaited sexual encounter, this one is heady with lust. Una's girlfriend Mollie has just brought Una to an orgasm, a release designed to ease Una's fears and create the spasms that may help the sperm swim upward. It's hard to come, but at last Una escapes into the release, thrashing around on the bed, and Mollie's grinning above her, semen and syringe at the ready. Una lies on her bed with her legs spread, heart racing, open, exposed, and vulnerable. She doesn't expect the first try to take, yet she can't help but be hopeful. The waiting and wondering is starting all over again in another way, but at last, she is really ready to begin. She opens her legs wider and prepares to let the heavens in.

WENDY ATKIN

Post-Partum Sex

AFTER A WOMAN HAS OPENED HER WOMB for the birth of a child, her sex life will ebb. Or at least this is the argument to be found in some books on female reproduction. A mother-to-be may be shocked to read that her love juices will dry up, or that a tiny baby will dominate her body with its physical demands. Breast-feeding can trigger a series of vaginal contractions, but these feel like an itch the mother cannot scratch and cannot be compared to the satisfaction a full orgasm brings.

Whoever wrote those books did not have a beautiful young lover like mine.

Our sexual adventures together did not diminish after childbirth. Becoming a mother did result in changes—my sleep deprivation is no longer the result of a long night fucking her over and over again. If I am seen walking around the house in various states of undress, it may be because the rush between diaper changes, feeding, and comforting times has afforded simply no time for me to get dressed. But the sexual side of my life did not slip out of the picture, as this illustration from a certain summer day suggests.

One hot day in July, with the early afternoon sun slanting through the bedroom blinds, I lie prostrate on the bed. My sticky skin conforms to that of my infant, damp in the heat, sucking on my left breast. A mother's arms lift many things in the course of a day—and night—and mine are sore. I have been awake since five a.m. with this demanding little being and I yearn to let my body drift into a restful state. So we nurse together, he and I, with the wish that both of us will nap through the heat of this summer afternoon.

Finally, his perfect pink lips let go and my nipple slips into the air, hot, wet, and red. I watch it cool, shrinking back to its hard pinkness, waiting out the moments when he slips deeply into sleep and my body twitches with fatigue, struggling against the activity my brain dictates.

But sleep deprivation wins out and my body relaxes. Just then my lover slips into the room, wearing that tight grey t-shirt I love. Her firm, tanned arms scoop our baby up without waking him and she motions toward the bathroom with her loving eyes. "Go, take a shower and make yourself feel good; I can handle this now." And she disappears through the door.

Not a bad idea. The skin on my body has layers of accumulated sweat, breast milk, and God knows what else. I ease myself under the warm water and arch my back to its spray. Amazing how sensuality is heightened in the period post-partum. Just the feel of my own body alone in this refreshing watery chamber hints at ecstasy.

But I am not alone for long. She enters the bathroom pulling off her shorts. She has barely put one muscular leg into the stall before bending at my waist and running her hands along my hips. "Did you always have such huge breasts?" she asks, pulling them around her face. I close my eyes, wondering if I have it in me to provide one more ounce of sustenance for another human being.

My breasts *are* huge. Swollen with milk, the nipples point straight ahead. They respond quickly to her tongue. She licks, teases, then to my surprise pulls the left tit wholly into her mouth. I gasp at the swift let-down. The milk flows into and around her beautiful red lips. I moan, and ask, "Do you like it—does it taste strange?" She gives me that long, dark look I've seen in her eyes before, and I know she is enjoying herself.

She pulls away and rises to eye level. Holding my head firmly between the palms of her hands, she asks, "Don't you know that mothers are the sexiest women?"

"No," I say, "I've never had one."

"Well, I'm lucky enough to have these," she moans, while pulling both of my breasts toward her glistening tongue.

I brace myself on the tiled wall. Warm water gushes down my shoulders. She *knows* the ecstatic effects of her hands gripping the sides of my tits, so her mouth can suck on two nipples at once.

She sucks furiously on both nipples at once. My knees buckle as the shock goes right to my clit. For an exquisite moment, only the wall and her mouth hold me up—then she lifts her face and milk streams out of my tits, while my hips sink into her palms. I gasp for air, poised on the brink of ultimate pleasure.

"It's alright," she soothes, reaching behind me and turning the water off with one hand. "Come on, come with me."

Taking a plush rose towel from the rack, she rubs me dry all over, then pulls me back to the bedroom. I'm like a child, collapsing in her strong arms. Exhausted, but happy, smooth, and warm, she holds me, then slips her fingers between my legs. My pussy is wet for her touch, aware that she knows just what to do.

"Now you have someone to take care of *you*," she whispers in my ear. My body rises against her palm. In fatigue my body is submissive to the waves of pleasure sent out by her fingers rubbing my clit. Although my senses are sleepy, the hand under my cunt is more insistent, and there is no doubt about where we are going. I come very quickly, my hip bones rising toward the ceiling in the final moan. Then I collapse into a deep, maternal sleep.

RACHEL ROSE

Sundays

"C'MERE AND SIT ON MY FACE," she says to me. "I wanna lick your pussy."

"No," I say, still reading my book. "I don't feel like it and I don't like it when you say pussy."

"Okay, keep reading, then. Just let me play with you a little."

I don't answer so she takes this as a yes. She tangles her fingers in the dark hair between my thighs. I should have put a robe on after my bath. She's still like this after three years together, can't leave me alone when I'm undressed. I'm holding a slim book of New Zealand Women Poets up to my face, but I am stuck on the same stanza, something about sheep and loneliness. I'm irritated, but more and more, I'm irritated because she's just teasing, just playing with the hair, not touching. I feel my cunt open and spread under her brushings. I press my face into the cool creamy pages of the book, breathing in ink and poetry. My breathing must have changed somehow, for I see a little smile play on the corners of her mouth, as though she knows she's won some kind of victory. Her brown eyes sparkle.

Unwilling to give up the illusion that I am still reading poetry, I turn the next page. But behind the book my eyes are closed, waiting for her tongue. With both hands she spreads my lips and inhales deeply. I am concentrating hard on holding completely still. She leaves me like that for an unbearably long time, spread open but unlicked, suffering under the warm air she breathes on me. I feel myself getting wet.

I am waiting for only one thing: her tongue on my clit. So when she presses a wet finger against my asshole, I gasp. She is still holding me spread. I can't resist a peak over the cover of my book. She spits in the direction of my asshole and her finger gathers up the liquid, rubs it across that tight brown muscle. I see and feel her press in, then back away, press in again and disappear between the cheeks of my ass.

I cover my face with the book. It feels very good, and yet my frustration is mounting as my clit is ignored. She doesn't speak. Her moves are slow, as though she doesn't want to disturb my reading.

But I am disturbed. I try to keep my hips still, but they start a motion of their own, small but irrepressible. My nails are denting the cover of my book and I have one creamy sheet of paper bent between my teeth. Stop it, I tell myself sternly. This is a library book. Finally with a groan I lift my hips up to her mouth and her tongue spreads over my clit and vibrates. I can feel the sweet rush of heat and blood between my legs, I can feel the orgasm building almost as soon as her tongue is on me, and still that finger pressing deeper and deeper into my ass. But when her other hand slides two fingers into my cunt I lose it, lifting my hips even higher and coming hard, hard, in her mouth.

After a while I lift the book off my face. There is a wet mark from my mouth across a poem about pioneers. I wipe my face and turn the page. She cradles her head on my thighs, breathing hard, her cheeks flushed a dusky pink. The short dark wisps of hair on her forehead and the nape of her neck curl softly with sweat. She falls asleep this way, and I turn the page and continue to read, one hand stroking her hair.

In the afternoon I come into the kitchen. She's wearing nothing but a tank top and cut-offs, and I can see the curves of her luscious, big ass as she washes dishes. Soap bubbles drip from her elbows, and the muscles of her arms shine with steam and sweat.

"C'mere, baby," I say. "I want you."

"No," she says, "I gotta do the dishes."

So I come up behind her and slowly work her shorts over her wide hips, down her belly.

"Don't mind me," I tell her, my hand slipping in front to finger her. "Don't mind me, I'm not really here."

J E A N N I E   W I T K I N

Paper or Plastic?

for Anna

YOU RAN YOUR FINGER ALONG the fine hairs at the back of my neck and my skin tingled all the way down my spine. Should I buy three apples, or four? Their skin is shiny, feels cold and smooth except for the furry part near the stem. Usually, I don't notice. But I was acutely aware, at the time, of the space between my chin and chest, because your mouth was pressed there. Your mouth is the warmest, wettest place in the world. Well no, I'm wrong, already forgetting. There's one warmer. But you ran your tongue across my neck and I could think of nothing else. Now I am focussed on cereal, raisin bran or corn flakes this week? The skin on my neck is only a place my sweatshirt goes around, nothing more. I know there was an instant when it was all important, but if I don't buy cereal I won't eat in the morning. What did you do to me last night that undid me so, shifted my priorities? Your hands on my body were everything, the universe stopped at the edge of my bed. Do other people do this, too? That woman, carefully looking over the tomatoes, has she ever moaned out loud, rumpled the covers, left stains on the sheet, sweated? Did she do it last night? If she did, if she remembers, how can she possibly decide which tomato will go best in tonight's fresh tossed salad? If I remember, suddenly, unbidden, images of your hand inside my body, plowing me, my stomach lurches. I must put out a hand to steady myself, overtaken with this physical rush, this sensation. You took me, possessed me, then gave me back to myself, and now I am faced with shelves of juice and I must decide which bottle to take home with me. What was it that caused me to make those high pitched moaning sounds in the back of my throat? How was I feeling that made it absolutely necessary to rake my nails across your back? Which loaf of bread is the freshest? What did I mean by that gesture? Why does everyone not spend every minute of every day in bed with someone else? Yet I have gone months, years even, without doing this. And, often, not minded. You show me, again and again, what my body is for, can do, wants, and the wanting is exponential. I want you, again, tonight. Do you want paper or plastic? No, sex. I want sex.

SUSAN HOLBROOK

Why do I feel so guilty in the lingerie department at The Bay

AFTER ALL, I'M A WOMAN, I'm old enough to look casual in here, I'm in my prime, in fact: why not try on a few things, discuss sizes and wires with the clerk like it's nothing, a bit of a chore even, like shopping for sneakers. The thing is I don't feel casual; I get seriously flushed around all these Vogue Playtex Daisyfresh girlies in their underwear on boxes the size of XXX videos. And today I see you in all the pictures. You're the one smiling off to the left in a flattering three-quarters pose, underwired, lace-trimmed, full-figured, in black, white or the lurid "nude." And I also see you in that emerald green satin bra that's slinking there loose in the bin, boxless. The bin is where the loose women get bras, women like me. "Brah," my mother used to say it, as in "brat," claiming "bra" as in "draw" was an affectation. Either way is an affectation if you ask me, a way to unpronounce desire, a big coverup. I walk over to the bin, my hand goes in. Yes, it's official, I want you in this emerald green satin bra, even though all you ever wear is a white sportsbra. Or sportsbrah. What if I bought it for you, maybe you'd go for it, maybe you'd give up your sportsbra for the evening. Nobody would have to know. Maybe nothing is more important today than spending whatever and easing you into this emerald green satin bra.

"Can I help you?" asks the saleswoman. She is my mother's age, pink silk blouse, black sweater vest, lipstick, 34 B, I think, before I can stop myself.

"Yes, I'm looking for socks," I want to say. But I've clearly been holding the green bra for a few minutes now, my clammy fingerprints all over it.

"Do you have this in a C-cup?" I ask.

Her eyes dart to my chest. "That's a little large probably, for you."

"Oh, it's not for me, it's for my sister-in-law," I say.

My cheek twitches with the lie, so it looks like I'm winking at her. That makes her uneasy. I notice she has a nametag that says Erma on it and a tape measure around her neck, which she now clutches at each end so that it cuts into her flesh like a bra strap that's too tight. There's no way she'll use the tape measure on me at this point. That's for people who are genuinely casual, people with plastic skin and stainless steel nipples, people who would never salivate or lose their breath or get wet under the scuff and tug of Erma's tape measure. My nice woman façade is cracking off in great hunks and Erma can see the dirty old pervert beneath. She looks stunned. Like she's at a loss as to how to protect all those bare-shouldered girls on the bra boxes from my leers, like she's about to call security. Or like she just realized, *Oh my god I work in the underwear department.*

Then you saunter in with your baseball cap and your gas station attendant jacket that says Jake and the Sportsmans you just bought in the men's department. You eye the green A-cups in my hand and assume they're for me, lick your lips and break the awkward silence with an *mmm* sound.

"Is this your brother?" asks a hopeful Erma, clearly more comfortable with incest than dykes. Or maybe she directs your desire toward the absent sister-in-law. That fictional sister-in-law who will make this sale respectable. Poor dear sister-in-law, she's really in need of this bra. Her little Jake says *mmm* and oop, there she goes through the daisy-fresh field of Erma's imagination, her breasts flopping around in a family values breeze, crying out for a little satin restraint.

"Mmm," I answer, and Erma retreats into the stockroom to get the C. But Brother Jake has got a hold of his sister, refusing to let me take my clammy A-cups back to the loosewoman bin. Looks like we're buying in bulk today. Going for the emerald green satin bra family pack. Maybe later we'll go home and give each other a fitting. Get out the tape measure and play lingerie store. I get to be Erma, and you can be the woman in her prime, getting a little flushed.

R I D D L E

Fill Me Up

I ADMIT IT. I WAS COCKY—laughing at my friends—"How could you let her have so much power over you?" And then you set your sights on me.

It started out just Sunday mornings—with friends—with or without conversations. Gradually it increased, one . . . two . . . three days a week . . . meeting alone. I thought I was in control, I thought I could handle you, but before I could blink, it was an everyday thing and I soon realized that you were the main reason I was getting out of bed every morning. It didn't matter what was going on, I had to see you—I didn't even care if I was late for work, which was starting to happen with greater frequency. I knew I was in too deep, I knew it had to end—so I told you, "It's over," casting myself into turmoil and chaos. But you, you just laughed knowing I'd be back, and you were right.

It's been about a month since I've held you, brought you in close to me, inhaling your scent deeply before taking you into my mouth and feeling the world melt away. Afterward, I'd always felt so strong, so capable, so alive! So I decided to come back—just this once.

I try to act so cool, so nonchalant, hands slightly twitching as I approach the counter.

"Double tall iced Americano, please."

"Room for cream?"

"Uh-huh," I practically whimper. And once again I am holding you, breathing you in, watching the cream fall into you, becoming one with you, as I know you will become one with me. And then you are in my mouth, bitter, smooth and oh, so cool. Technically I am the consumer but I know that I am being consumed. You flow down into my limbs, the colour has come back into the world. As I walk out the doors, your energy flowing through my veins, you know that I have always been yours and that I'll be back again, tomorrow.

MEREDITH ROSE

A Machine Called Betty

IT WAS NOT LOVE AT FIRST SIGHT. Call it something else: curiosity, amusement, infatuation, fascination, desire. But it was not love.

Clarice was not a wealthy woman. She had no trust fund to fall back on, only the black futon couch which she made into a bed each night before she fell to sleep and dreamed of lovers past, present, and future.

Clarice was not broke, but she had to be careful with her money. She was a smart shopper. She knew how to cut corners, but she was also a woman of fine aesthetic sensibilities who took pleasure in sensuous and sensual delights—a woman who loved to make love; a woman who loved a dirty fuck. She was a lesbian. She was complex.

Now Clarice was in trouble. In the catalogues and pamphlets she was assured that a love like this could never be, would never be. And yet. . . .

Clarice could not afford the Hitachi Wand or the Panabrator. She had no money for the Oster Stick Massager. So instead, three weeks ago on an overcast Wednesday after work, she drove her Dodge Dart to a nearby mall and made her way to the Domestic Wares aisle of the K-Mart shopping centre. On the top shelf, next to a row of shower heads, Clarice found what she was looking for. It was electrically operated, included assorted attachments, had a full one-year warranty, and most importantly, it was on sale.

At home, Clarice sliced through the cellophane wrapping with a butter knife and opened the cardboard box. She carried her new vibrator into her bedroom and closed the door.

From six until nine p.m., on the hour and half-hour, Clarice's lover telephoned leaving messages, her tone increasing with urgency from a neutral "Hello, sweetie. Give me a call when you get in," to a desperate, "Where the fuck are you? You said you'd be home, goddammit!"

Clarice was unaware. On striped percale sheets she came and came, and then came again.

With each night that passed, Clarice's fondness for her vibrator grew. It was intense, it was dependable, but it was only a machine. It lacked certain tender qualities. It did not call out Clarice's name as she released herself; nor did it bring her a cool cloth, or rub her body with oil of almond.

But now she was in trouble, because those intimate things didn't seem to matter as much anymore and Clarice's lover, whom Clarice loved, felt betrayed and demanded an explanation.

"Her name," Clarice's lover had shouted, "tell me her fucking name!"

"Betty," Clarice had blurted out, as her lover bit back tears. "But it's not what you think."

Her lover slammed the front door as she ran out. Clarice flopped back on the futon. She removed Betty from her cardboard box and plugged her in.

Though they said it couldn't happen, the truth was Clarice had fallen in love with a machine called Betty.

JULES TORTI

Marge Simpson, My Blue Angel

MARGE SIMPSON, SUCH AN EXQUISITE BEAUTY. Dressed simply in her favourite guacamole green dress, accented with a string of bright red pearls and matching heels, she is absolutely smashing. Her stack of brilliant blue hair standing neat and erect upon her cartoon head, large, innocent eyes, a husky voice, I am swept *away to the land of dream*.

Marge, what's under that spumoni green one-piece? Are you all smooth down there like Ken and Barbie? Do you have a little blue bird? Wiry, Smurf-blue curls? I've never made love to a woman with blue pubic hair. Perhaps you are somewhat darker in your erogenous zone. I know natural blondes who are actually brunette between their legs. Maybe you're not Smurf-blue, but navy instead.

Marge, I want to pet your sweet blue bird and make it sing *"zippidy-do-dah, zippidy-deh, my, oh my, what a wonderful day. . . ."* At night, I find myself imagining you and I under silk leopard-skin sheets. You are naked except for your treasured red pearls; your pistachio pudding green skirt is but a wrinkled heap on the purple shag carpet.

Tonight, you wear your wondrous hair down, abandoning the blow dryer and usual fixatives. I would love it down. I would love how it would cradle your beautiful, supple breasts and tickle the small of your back. Are your nipples blue too, Marge?

I would love to seduce you. I would slip you out of that dress and explore every inch of your neglected body. In my dreams, you step out of the shower (*don't worry, Homer's not home, he took the kids bowling*) smelling of rich, intoxicating Body Shop products. *Mmmm.* Invigorating green apple shower gel—fruity, with just a bite of ginger. I dry you off with practiced hands. Your hair smells sweet, like ripe tangerines. I nuzzle your neck and enjoy the seductive woody scent of sea kelp, agave and Chinese peony.

I lure you into the bedroom where several vanilla candles have been lit. Two tall flutes of Giacomo Borgogno have been placed beside the bed. You carefully reach for a glass and lower your nose close to the rim. We both absorb the firm notes of truffles and leather in a deep breath.

"Barolo Riserva, 1990?"

I am impressed with your knowledge of Italian reds. I nod my head, smiling.

"Excellent selection," you commend, in your sensuous, raspy voice.

We take appreciative sips, our senses heightened with the anticipation of the evening before us. You notice the delicate white rose I have placed on your pillow. You caress its fine petals and offer a warm, knowing smile. You place the rose on the walnut night table beside your wedding photo, which you turn face down.

I place my hand on your slender waist. "Wait," you whisper. I watch as you move elegantly across the room, your silk mauve robe open at the front, revealing your irresistible body. Poetry without words. You hold up a CD. Of course. I had forgotten, my head and heart were already full of song.

Ahhh. A perfect choice, Marge. A timeless classic, Pachelbel's *Canon* in D major. You return to the bedside and immediately drop your robe, your carnal desires overwhelming any conscious thought. Just as I'd suspected, your hard nipples are deep sea blue, your pubic hair navy. "Let me give you a massage," I insist—worried that I will rush our precious moments together. You accept by lying down on your stomach, smiling devilishly.

The massage oil is a stimulating blend of rose and patchouli. I begin with soft, careful strokes, tracing your body's natural curves. I apply more concentrated pressure, much to your approval, working from the small of your back up to your neck. I continue, gradually feeling the tension in your shoulders disappear. I move down your spine, choosing to linger on your lumbar and then proceed to your buttocks. Two soft, baby blue malleable cheeks, perfectly rounded like balls of plastercine. You enjoy the deep penetration of your tender muscle tissue. I watch as one hand mischievously disobeys my conscience and slips into your cleft, brushing lightly against your little rose. With a deliberate touch, I feel it contract, inviting and begging my entry.

You moan in satisfied delight as I push the full length of my finger inside you. I begin with a circular motion, and then, in response to your body's reaction, gentle thrusts. You rub your wet labia forcefully against my bare knee as I remain kneeling behind your buttocks. The rhythm we share creates a chorus for the *Canon*.

I remove my finger slowly and slide along the sheets to your side. Immediately, you mount me, pressing your burning pelvis and aching body into my own. Our hungry bodies ride the waves of passion, rocking like a boat swept out into the stormy sea.

Your bouncing pearls tickle the sensitive nape of my neck as I feel the palm of your hand firmly against my inner thigh. You move deftly up my leg and tease me with a soft stroke, circling the pearl of my sexual universe, my clitoris swollen with desire. You press suggestively against my opening, and my body consumes you completely. You slip in and out while your thumb concentrates on my clit. I cannot resist. I plunge into your blue bird and massage your warm walls, encouraging your womanly syrup to flow.

Thrusting and grinding, we increase to a quick vibrato. I feel your hot, sugary breath on my neck. Your fingers dig into my back and I am breathless. We come simultaneously, our bodies conquered.

"You are my Sappho in pearls," I whisper to Marge, "a precious blue angel." Running my fingers through her lovely Smurf-blue hair I kiss her sweet lips. I close my eyes and sink into the whirlpools of post-orgasmic bliss, humming.

"Zippidy-do-dah, zippidy-deh, my, oh my, what a wonderful day. . . ."

S A M M I   F R E E Z E

Just Passing Through

A QUICK LOOK, BEFORE I STEP IN. Great, they *are* in full uniform here. It adds a delicious sharpness, a slight edge, to the tiny jaws holding on so lovingly, the liquid metal tickle. Every step a pull, every movement bringing me closer.

First stop. Drop the bag, knowing that it will sail through with flying colours. The problem is me. I turn the corner, show my pass. Nothing for the dish, at least nothing that I plan on offering. But I throw a shrug into my response, inhaling sharply from the cold steel where none should be.

Now for that moment, and my luck holds. I face a woman. And she is so butch: the crease razor sharp on her regulation pants, black boots polished to a high shine, her white shirt without a wrinkle. And a tie—she doesn't *have* to wear a tie. Sure does look good on her, though. Blonde hair just a tad long, carefully slicked back. Blue, blue eyes, squinting somewhat, giving her that distant, superior look.

No turning back now. I step through, time slowing down until I can count my heartbeats—loud to my ears—can feel the blood pulsing through me. Of course, as I ease through the gate, it beeps.

She motions me forward with a flip of her hair. Catching her glance, I show off the flush across my face and throat, pursing my full lips slightly, taking short, shallow breaths. She calmly slides the wand down in front of my torso, its high beep drawing her eyes to my very erect nipples under a black silk blouse. She hesitates for a brief moment: What is her wand sensing?

Stalling for time, she passes slowly down the front of each leg, rises and taps a shoulder to turn me around. A long sweep downward, but no more beeps. Another tap and I am staring into her eyes again, barely in control of myself, her careful attention to the job more than I could hope for. I allow myself a slight shimmy as the wand passes across my front once more. It is enough—my cunt pulses in time with my chained nipples. Her eyes darken as she drinks in my shudder. With a deep inhale through flared nostrils, and an appreciative smirk, she waves me through.

JUDITH QUINLAN

A Love Story

Fatima had the best dildo I've ever had the pleasure to . . . well, the pleasure. She said she bought it in Bath eleven years ago, and doesn't remember its name. We'd been sleeping together for a month when she first introduced it to me. After that I couldn't get enough of it. Or her, of course. It wasn't particularly fancy or anything. Just your basic silicone dill, in putrid orange, with a small base. It had little horizontal ridges starting about halfway down the wider bulbous end, then it smoothed and narrowed, then it widened again at the base, had a bit of a bend and was offset from the centre of the base. The tip was slightly softer that the stem. It was similar to lots of other dildos. But somehow this little baby was exactly right for me. It just fit.

Fatima and I enjoyed each other's company in bed and elsewhere for the better part of a year, then she decided to move to Rotterdam, and I wasn't ready to make that sort of a commitment, but it was a close thing. I tried to get custody of the dildo. She got cute and said it would be an incentive for me to visit. Like I'd ever have enough money to visit Rotterdam. I offered a half-share arrangement—she'd get the dildo on months with odd numbers of days, and I'd get even. She didn't go for it. So I took the train as far as Montreal to see her off at the airport. We cried. We promised to write. That's the last I saw of the best dildo I've ever known.

I tried, after that, to find another like it. I did research into all the silicone dildo factories—not that many, after all, but the problem is that a lot of them started out as collectives. So nobody has any idea who did what or when. Simple facts that should be part of any company's record-keeping were relegated to the realm of folklore. ("That was when Maryann was sleeping with a man and before the stock-room fire.") Or even if somebody knew somebody who worked there back then, she was in Greece in serious retreat. I put ads in women's magazines and lesbian newspapers, offering outrageous rewards to anyone who could find me a dill just like the dill that . . . well, you get the idea. But it seems that after Fatima's little beauty was born, they broke the mold. Literally, they did. Because I finally found out it was manufactured by the Dreaming Dawn Dildo Co-operative, in Lansing, Michigan, and only one pouring (twenty-five dills) was done. Then Rowena, who had been having a clandestine affair with the bookkeeper, Gerty (clandestine so that Rowena's partner, Jan, wouldn't know), found out that Gerty had been sleeping with Sal who was their best dildo mold-maker, and Rowena lost her cool and smashed the mold by tossing it under the wheels of an approaching tractor trailer. The driver of this rig, it turned out, was an ex-rodeo queen from Tucson, Carly-Ann, and Rowena eventually went into partnership with her as the now-famous "Mother Truckers," America's first all-dyke long distance haulers. Sal and Jan ended up running a bed and breakfast in Tecumseh, specializing in bird-watching gays, which is where I finally ran them to ground and found out that if I ever wanted a taste of my favourite dildo, I had two choices: to move to Rotterdam, or sleep with Gerty, who had possession of Sal's original prototype. It's even the same putrid orange. Gerty moved to Winnipeg after the Molotov cocktail scandal at Dreaming Dawn, and got a job keeping books for the Winnipeg Symphony. Then she moved to Yellowknife and freelanced, which wasn't too lucrative, but she'd fallen in love with a dogsled racer who had her heart set on the Iditerod. When that relationship went belly-up, so to speak, in the land of the midnight sun, she packed her leftover puppy and down parkas down to Penticton, which is where I'd been living with Fatima when this whole thing started. So there she was, and there I was, and there was the double of Fatima's dildo, and nobody was getting any younger, and so on.

This time I intend to negotiate a custody agreement early on in the relationship. I'll wait a bit. I don't want Gerty thinking I only love her for her dildo. That would be ridiculous. Of course I love her for who she is.

JUDITH KATZ

History Lessons

YOU WERE THE NEW DYKE IN TOWN, Nadine. Me, Rose Shapiro, I brought you there myself. In my own arms with my own hands, although at the time I was myself under water, the underwater life I made by rolling sticky green pot between thin sheets of paper and smoking it like some grade-B movie lesbirado. But I remember your arrival as if it happened yesterday. The story goes like this.

I was driving back from Cambridge at three in the morning with a pound of homegrown Vermont sinsemilla which I purchased from my friends Verna and Leslie in order to sell it to the dykes of New Chelm to help get them high and also pay my rent. I sampled the pot and sampled it some more and by the time I finally picked my smoky way out of Boston, I had given up all hope of ever seeing the Mass. Pike or any of my girlfriends in New Chelm again. So you can imagine my relief when I finally saw a sign that said Route 9 and remembered from my frequent trips back and forth across the state for purposes of buying high-grade lesbonic weed for the good of the people that if I followed it west, Route 9 would take me all the way into the tiny town of my home, New Chelm.

One look at any map will show that an inevitability of Route 9 is the city of Worcester, of which I can say not one good thing. Except, that is where I found the hero of our story, the aforementioned—you, Nadine Pagan.

On that night, Nadine, you looked like a wolf if ever I saw one. You stood with your thumb out under a streetlight in a flannel shirt, jeans, and high-tops, your wild hairs tied back to make you look like a boy, but I wasn't fooled. Years of looking at women in moonlight showed your true self to me. I pulled over and pushed open the door of my little bug and into it you slid.

You are a small woman, but there was a heaviness to you then, Nadine. Not a heft, but a great weight that seemed to be lodged firmly on your slight shoulders. You wore a knapsack and carried a violin case which you put carefully on your lap like some baby. Then you bundled my twisted seat belt around you both and stared straight ahead.

"Where are you going?" I asked. I was tempted to give you a lecture about the dangers of middle-of-the-night hitchhiking for women, but here I was with a Volkswagen full of marijuana, stoned out of my mind, so really, who was I to talk?

You turned your face to me, and there in the street lamp light I saw it, that big purple ring around your face that was your face. I gulped a little because it was awesome and I reached my fingers to touch it but stopped short because—did you flinch? Did you duck? Did I remember that I was a lesbian and were you one or not? How could I know? Instead I put a hand on the steering wheel of my little yellow bug, let out the clutch, and we were on our way into the woods that stretched between dreaded Worcester and home.

"I don't care where you are going," you said in a voice that sounded like fingernails running down a chalkboard. "I have nothing to lose."

I twisted the radio dial this way and that until I found something that sounded like music. The pickings were slim as it was far into the middle of the night and we were in Worcester after all. But now, with you my companion, it became a fine night to travel. I rolled down the window on my side and realized I knew this road and, better yet, how to get off it and on to a more magical one. And so, with a flip of my blinker and a turn of my wheel we began to sail through the beautiful and curving roads that brought us from Worcester to Ware to Belchertown, New Salem and points west, with rises and falls, dips and turns, until finally we crossed the concrete bridge that carried us over the Chelm River into the New Chelm Valley and up the rickety alley of a street that was the centre of town.

"This is where the journey ends," I told you. "I live down that street over there. Do you have a place to stay?"

You unlocked your seat belt and gathered your violin to you. You looked with your ringed face into my own and leaned toward me. Then, with a fierce glint in your eye, you kissed me on the mouth. Oh, Nadine, I was yours from that minute on.

The love we made was animal. Biting, chewing, untrimmed fingernail sex, sex that scratched and pulled me in the wrong places, but how could I say no? These were the early days of public lesbian life. No one was even sure if they knew the right way to go down on someone, let alone talk about it or ask for it a different way. We had sore cunt sex at its most enjoyable, the kind I thought about two days later and my cunt clenched, my knees got weak, and I couldn't wait to be biting and sucking and chewing you again.

I know now I was your first woman lover but I couldn't tell that then. I was marveling because your enthusiasm and clumsiness were no different than that of the other six women I'd been with so far. What was different was your passion, Nadine, which was wider and stretched me further than any of my other lovers. And a sorrow that I sensed just under your snarly surface, a sadness so vast it begged me to jump into it and soothe you. I wanted you more than any of those other women, who were sweet enough and smart enough but never quite poked at my heart the way you did. You were so far away so much of the time, Nadine, but I viewed you then as I view you now—my first and truest love.

How did you manage to come out while you were living with your grandmother or with such a dark scar etched into your crazy face? Did you plod through the card catalogues in the Worcester Public Library to find books about lesbians, homosexuality, inversion, and deviance? Did you wolf around the one gay bar in Worcester to find others like you? I still don't know, and in those days I never thought to ask.

I just figured based on how you kissed me that you always had and always would be a lesbian like all the other dykes I knew by then. Before you came around I was kind of a big shot, one of the famous New Chelm lezzies who came out in an undergraduate clump over at the university. I was in charge of refreshments, provided lovely weed and exotic trips that came on squares of blotter paper, tools to make the dancing easy. Those were the days! How we rubbed each others' backs and got crazy jealous and high. How we horrified ourselves by tossing our ex-lovers' keys down the sewer right before their eyes, or sleeping with someone one night and then not speaking to them for months, maybe years after. How we marveled in the taste and pull and differences in each others' spicy cunts.

By the time I brought you to my bed, Nadine, I was already part of the five-year dyke club. Had my own room in the New Chelm lesbian rooming house on Vick Street, my own collection of lesbian tracts and theories, and a dozen posters on my walls, all artifacts of our new-forming lesbo archaeology. Dated and lovely ornaments of our earliest struggles to locate not only others like us, but even ourselves.

I never questioned your credentials, Nadine. The fact of your landing your mouth on mine just an hour after I met you was proof enough of your queerness for me.

I got you a room down the hall from my own in the Vick Street house. To call it a room is generous. It was in fact a gable with enough floor space to contain the thin piece of foam that was your bed, your music stand, and the world's tiniest desk. You kept your clothes rolled up in balls and tangles in the cubby that passed for a closet. It was lucky you had hardly any possessions and no one to visit but me.

In those days. as you know, I supplemented my pot-selling income by working as a prep cook and cashier at New Chelm's dyke restaurant, *Lechem V'Shalom*, a Hebrew name that translated into Bread and Peace—in any language, two necessities of life. It was an enjoyable job which met all my social needs. Through those doors, six days a week, practically every dyke in the world came for herb teas or soups full of the vegetables I chopped with my own two hands, eggs over easy, potato latkes, black beans and rice, or any of the other delicacies of vegetarianism we collectively rotating cooks might provide.

You took a job as dishwasher at *Lechem V'Shalom,* first for free meals and then for the small cheque that paid your rent (twenty-seven dollars a week) and provided some extra for the necessities of your life, which included, among other things, tampons, violin strings, paper, and pens.

It was hard work to get you that job, bottom of the lesbian pile though it was. Because your voice was tightly strung you hardly spoke, and some women thought you mute. Because your wild hairs flew out from every side of your purple scar with a Health Department-regulated *babushka* tied around your head, some suspected you were berserk. The scar itself made you monstrous to some, and for these reasons you were relegated to the back of the restaurant with the garbage and cracked plates. It was months before you proved yourself sane enough to wield a knife against carrots and onions, green beans and tomatoes, in the society of our kitchen.

Yet through this all, you seemed almost cheerful. You slept into the morning, wandered the streets of New Chelm for exercise, then went back to your little room and played on your violin for hours and hours until it was time to make your way to the back door of the restaurant. You ate your dinner, then paid it off by spraying down dishes and shoving them into the washer. Then you came out to the back stoop to smoke a hand-rolled (tobacco) cigarette with me, emptied the clean dishes, and started all over again.

We hardly spoke at the end of those nights, but still, I loved you better than all my other girlfriends. As we strolled back up to Vick Street, a lit joint passing between us, there were times when for no reason at all you started to laugh like the maniac most of New Chelm feared you to be. But that didn't bother me, Nadine. I loved how we'd holler up to the top floor of the rooming house because neither of us remembered our key. Before long, some dyke or other in a flannel shirt and a pair of overalls, with hardly any hair and a crabby disposition, came to let us in. When together, usually in giggles, we made our way up the creaky stairs and into my bed, we had more sore cunt sex, more laughing and howling, until one or both of us fell asleep. I was determined to let my other lovers go. I dreamed of a life with you alone, Nadine, the two of us ragged outlaws against the rest of the whole sad world.

LESLÉA NEWMAN

The Days to Come

IF IT'S TUESDAY, THIS MUST BE . . . Shannon. Lori opened one eye and peered through the darkness. Yep, that was Shannon, all right. Lori could tell by the bald head crowning between her legs. Like a baby, she thought. "That's good, honey, a little harder now. That's it, Ja—I mean, Shannon."

Shannon stopped for a nanosecond, and then pressed Lori's clit harder against her tongue. Lori smiled. Calling any lover by the wrong name always made them work a little harder. It reminded them there was stiff competition—no pun intended, as Jackie and Gloria were the only ones who used dildoes. Shannon had balked at the idea. "See these?" She wiggled her ten fingers. "Sex toys." Precisely the reason Lori was a die-hard believer in non-monogamy.

Shannon stuck in two—or was it three?—of her "sex toys" into Lori's cunt and thrust them in and out while she licked Lori's clit clean. Lori let go, screaming, "Oh!" in one long, loud cry of pleasure. With Shannon it was "Oh!," with Jackie it was "Ah!," and with Gloria it was "Oy!" because Gloria's turn came on Friday nights when the two nice Jewish girls played "Sabbath Bride" together.

Shannon withdrew her fingers and rested her head on Lori's right thigh, enoying the sensations rippling through her own body. Lori's

"Big Oh!" never failed to cause her cunt to clench and her clit to explode but she never inched her way up Lori's body to kiss her on the mouth in gratitude. Shannon kissed only Jackie's mouth, Gloria's breasts, and Lori's cunt. That way, she remained faithful to each of her girls in her own way. Besides, "Leave them wanting more" was always a good way to go. Shannon knew she satisfied Lori, but that Lori would do anything—anything!—for a sweet, chaste, goodnight kiss on the mouth. Shannon could make Lori come (and come and come) by pulling, pinching, squeezing, sucking, licking, and biting her breasts, but Gloria lived for the day Shannon would go down on her ("Someday, baby, I'm just not ready yet"). And Jackie. Shannon could (and frequently did) say to Jackie, "You're the only girl I ever kiss," and it would not be a lie.

Scruples were important to Shannon. As they were to Lori, who never actually revealed the names of their lovers to each other. As they were to both Jackie and Gloria, which is why the double dildo they were both riding with pleasure at this very moment was covered with latex. Jackie's other lovers never used the "Daily Double," as she called it, even though she tried to convince them of its merits with that old chewing gum jingle: "Double your pleasure, double your fun. . . ." Still, it was best to play safe. Who wanted to worry at a time like this? Besides, Jackie had not given up hope that someday Shannon would get over her "Toys are for kids" attitude, and Lori would get over her "Real dykes only use strap-ons" fixation.

But Jackie wasn't even thinking about Lori and Shannon now. She was totally focussed on Gloria. The two women sat face to face, their arms and legs wrapped around each other, their hips pushing up and down in a slow, even, exquisite rhythm, their weight perfectly balanced like two girls on a seesaw. Gloria closed her eyes and let her hands cup Jackie's breasts, so much fuller than Shannon's, so much smaller than Lori's. She briefly wondered what each of her other lovers were doing at that very moment, but soon her body pulled her attention back to the here and now. Not only did she and Jackie come together, but their cries were simultaneous (not to mention in perfect harmony) with Shannon and Lori's, who were in the middle of their own second coming on the other side of town.

Hours later, all four women were in their own beds, asleep with smiles on their faces. Lori, still smelling of Shannon's cologne, dreamt of Jackie while she slept next to Iris. Shannon, a cunt hair of Lori's stuck in her teeth, dreamt of Gloria while she snored next to Meryl. Gloria, with Jackie's lipstick on her neck, dreamt of Shannon while she snoozed next to Roberta. Jackie, whose palms were still dusted with Gloria's sweat, dreamt of Lori while she snuggled next to Paula. Paula dreamed about Roberta who dreamed about Meryl who dreamed about Iris who dreamed about Paula. And in the days to come, all of their dreams would come true.

CONTRIBUTORS

Donna Allegra's work has been featured in *Best Lesbian Erotica 1997*, edited by Tristan Taormino and Jewelle Gomez; *Hers*, edited by Terry Wolverton; *The Wild Good*, edited by Beatrix Gates; *Does Your Mama Know?: An Anthology of Black Lesbian Coming-Out Stories*, edited by Lisa Moore; and *Queer View Mirror 1* and *2*.

Dorothy Allison is the author of *Bastard Out of Carolina*; *Skin: Talking About Sex, Class, and Literature*; *Two or Three Things I Know for Sure*; and *Trash*.

Odette Alonso is a poet and prose writer with a B.A. in Philology. Her poetry books *Enigma de la sed* (1989), *Historias para el desayuno* (1989), and *Palabra del que vuelve* (1996), were published in Cuba. Her work has also been included in several poetry anthologies. She now lives in Mexico City.

Red Jordan Arobateau is the author of forty books chronicling dyke life from the 1950s to 1990s, including *Lucy & Mikey, Street Fighter*, and a series of dyke biker books, published by Masquerade. Christian believer in the Mother God. Parent to cat colony. Married to dancer Dalila Jasmin for eleven years.

Wendy Atkin lives in Ottawa and writes fiction for her loved ones when not otherwise occupied as an advocate and researcher of child care policies in Canada.

L.K. Barnett is a twenty-three-year-old writer. She has contributed to *Lesbian Short Fiction*, *Does Your Mama Know: An Anthology of Black Lesbian Coming Out Stories*, and the forthcoming anthologies *On The Verge: Lesbian Tales of Power and Play* and *Looking Home*, both edited by Susan Fox Rogers.

Russel Baskin grew up in London, England before making Vancouver her home. She divides her time between her own art practice, writing and teaching creative process to youths and adults. Russel also works for "Outlook," a queer TV show. Her writing appears in *Queer View Mirror 2*.

Susan M. Beaver is a Mohawk from Six Nations, a member of the wolf clan. Her work appears in *Gatherings VIII* (Theytus), *Piece of My Heart* (Sister Vision), and *The Colour of Resistance* (Sister Vision). She is writing a novel that also has lots of water and sex in it.

Persimmon Blackbridge is the author of *Sunnybrook: A True Story With Lies*, which won the 1997 Ferro-Grumley Award for Fiction. Her latest novel *Prozac Highway* was selected as one of *The Advocate*'s top ten books of 1997. A writer, sculptor, and performance artist, she is a member of the Kiss & Tell Collective which produced the Lambda Award-winning book *Her Tongue on My Theory* and *Drawing the Line*. She lives in Vancouver.

Lucy Jane Bledsoe is the author of the novel *Working Parts* and of *Sweat: Stories and a Novella*, which was a Lambda Literary Award Finalist, and of two novels for young people, *Tracks in the Snow* and *The Big Bike Race*.

T.J. Bryan, a.k.a. Precious, lives in Toronto and is an attitudinal, Bajan, butch-lovin', dyke Creatrix. She has been published in *Matriart, Fireweed, Eye Wuz Here* (Douglas & McIntyre), *Queer View Mirror 2*, and *This Magazine*. A co-founder of De Poonani Posse's *Da Juice!,* she is also production manager and an editor of *Fireweed.*

Johanne Cadorette is a proud graduate school drop-out who will never quit her job at the bookstore because it provides her with a vibrant, stimulating social life. She is also a freelance writer, book reviewer, radio host, and emcee at large. She lives in Montréal.

Miriam Carroll, fast approaching sixty-eight, is loathe to let a day pass without filling it with creative purpose. Thus, she is exploring dance, acting, community involvement, outdoor activities, music, art, and writing.

tatiana barona de la tierra is a boss-bitch with a passion for rocks & writing & revolution. Born in Colombia, she zooms the cosmos with bullet-proof vulnerability. tatiana is editor of *Conmoción*, an international bilingual publication for latina lesbians all over.

Maria de los Rios—Cuban-Venezuelan dyke, served as member of the editorial board of the Latina lesbian magazine *Conmoción*. Published poetry, fiction, and non-fiction in *Conmoción*, *Revista Mujeres*, *Coquibacoa* (Women's Press), and *Yellow Leaves* (Burning Bush Press).

Nisa Donnelly is the author of two novels, *The Love Songs of Phoenix Bay* and the Lambda Award-winning *The Bar Stories: A Novel After All*, both from St. Martin's Press, and most recently the editor of the anthology *My Mother* (Alyson). She lives and writes in San Francisco.

Elana Dykewomon is the author of *Beyond the Pale*. Her classic novel *Riverfinger Women* (1974), one of the first lesbian novels published by a women's press in North America, was recently reissued by Naiad. She is the author of several books, including *Nothing Will Be As Sweet As the Taste, They Will Know Me By My Teeth,* and *Fragments From Lesbos*. She was the editor of *Sinister Wisdom*, an international journal for the lesbian imagination, for nine years.

Sammi Freeze surrounds herself with books, writing erotica late at night when lover and daughter are sleeping. A friend coined her name when mailing Sammi her first dildo. Sammi dreams of the day when she can escape her small rural community in eastern Canada to visit a sex club in San Francisco.

Emily George, born in 1944, is a radical lesbian feminist writer, political activist, performer, and grandmother who enjoys walking on stilts, painting pictures, and directing older women in circus performances.

Gabrielle Glancy's work has appeared in numerous journals and anthologies including *The New Yorker*, *The Paris Review*, *The Harvard Gay & Lesbian Review*, *Sister and Brother,* and *Queer View Mirror 1* and *2*. She is currently living in Tel Aviv and is at work on a novel.

Terrie Akemi Hamazaki is a Barracuda Femme living in Vancouver, Canada. She is a spiritual healer and writer/performance artist whose signature piece, "*Furusato* (Birth Place)," appears in *My Mother*.

Spike Harris lives and works in Vancouver. This is her first published piece of writing.

Susan Holbrook lives in Vancouver, where she writes and teaches and recovers from completing a Ph.D. in contemporary poetics at the University of Calgary. One day she would like to find a pair of emerald green satin Sportsmans.

Judith Katz is the author of two novels, *The Escape Artist* (Firebrand, 1997) and *Running Fiercely Toward a High Thin Sound* (Firebrand, 1992), from which "History Lessons" has been excerpted. *Running Fiercely* won a Lambda Literary Award for Best Lesbian Fiction. Her work has been widely anthologized in collections including *The Penguin Book of Women's Humor* and *Tasting Life Twice*.

Maureen King, fifty-seven years of age, is growing old disgracefully. Maureen is in her final stages of editing her first lesbian book, *The Journey*.

K. Linda Kivi is a mountain-dwelling, house-building, dykely babe of Estonian origin. Her publications include *Canadian Women Making Music,* the novel *If Home is a Place*, and the chapbook *Macho Sluts Build a House*. She is still looking for a publisher for her collection of slutty stories, *Living at Random*. "Moonriders" was first published in *Sinister Wisdom*.

Lydia Kwa lives and works in Vancouver as a writer and a psychologist. Her first book, a collection of poetry, *The Colours of Heroines*, was published by Toronto's Women's Press in 1994.

Marlys La Brash enjoys long rides on her motorcycle, volunteer work, and taking evening classes. Her sense of humour is evident in her cartooning. She is forty-one years young, single, and resides with her cat, Garfield, in Vancouver.

Fiona Lawry is a visual artist who often uses text and image in her work; creating provocative, erotic, and powerful works of art.

Rosalyn Sandra Lee has a degree in architecture and works as a facilities planner and is also proficient with computers. She wrote poetry many years ago and has recently rediscovered the words inside of her. She's currently working on two poetry manuscripts and several other short stories.

Susan Lee lives in Toronto. Her poetry has been recently published in Sister Vision's anthology, *But Where Are You Really From? Writings on Identity and Assimilation in Canada*, edited by Hazelle Palmer.

Denise Nico Leto is a San Francisco Bay Area poet, writer, and editor. Her work has appeared in many publications including *Writing for Our Lives*. She is currently working on a manuscript of poetry and a book of creative non-fiction.

Maria V. Mandulova is a twenty-five-year-old woman, born in Povdiv, Bulgaria, where homosexuality is still treated by many as a disease of the mind and a threat to society. She has studied English Language and Literature at the Plovdiv University and takes a great interest in foreign languages. She has a woman with a beautiful mind for her lover and hopes one day it will be possible for them to live together.

Mary Midgett, the Leo, writes short stories and is the author of *Brown on Brown: Black Lesbian Erotica*. She was featured in Tee Corinne's anthology of erotic writing called *Riding Desire*. Midgett the "sexpert" is also an erotic performer.

Rita Montana writes fiction and poetry. This is her first short short story to be published. Her poetry has appeared in various journals. Currently, she lives with her lover, their two dogs, Augie and Jolie, and Sasha, the cat.

Shani Mootoo is the author of *Cereus Blooms at Night*, which was shortlisted for the B.C. Book Prize for Fiction, the Chapters/*Books in Canada* First Novel Award, and the Giller Prize. She is the author of a short-story collection, *Out On Main Street*, and is also a multi-media visual artist and video-maker whose painting and photo-based works have been exhibited internationally.

Merril Mushroom is a frequent contributor to lesbian anthologies and periodicals.

Joan Nestle is the author of *A Restricted Country*, and the co-editor of the Lambda Award-winning *Sister and Brother: Lesbians and Gay Men Write About Their Lives Together,* and *Women on Women 1, 2* and *3*.

Lesléa Newman has published twenty-seven books, including *The Femme Mystique*, *The Little Butch Book*, *My Lover is a Woman: Con-*

temporary Lesbian Love Poems, and *Pillow Talk: Lesbian Stories Between the Covers.*

Anna Nobile is a writer and journalist living in Vancouver. Her work has appeared in such journals as *the eyetalian, effe* and *The Antigonish Review.* She is a regular contributor to *Angles* Magazine and was a key organizer for Write Out West, Canada's first lesbian, gay, bisexual, and transgender writers' conference.

Sharon Noble is a native of New York now residing in Los Angeles. She continues to read her erotic work at many lesbian events. She is a facilitator of a women's writing collective. Her latest accomplishments include *Lesbian Bedtime Stories*, an audio recording of lesbian erotica.

August Noir is a dyke writer who has been to a sex club only once.

Laura Panter is a twenty-seven-year-old self-employed business owner living in Toronto. Her works have appeared in *The Queen's Feminist Review*, and *Queer View Mirror 1* and 2. She is currently working on several plays and is plotting her first novel.

Gerry Gomez Pearlberg is the editor of *Queer Dog: Homo/Pup/Poetry* (Cleis), an anthology of canine poetry by lesbian and gay poets, and the author of *Marianne Faithfull's Cigarette*, a book of poems due out in 1998. She is at work on a novel.

Rachel Pepper may well be pregnant by the time you read this story. She will be growing bigger by the minute behind the counter of her bookstore, Bernal Books, in San Francisco, perusing baby name books.

Judith Quinlan lives at Sky Ranch, 140 acres of open women's land in northern British Columbia. She publishes *The Open Door*, a newsletter for rural lesbians and feminists. Her work has been published in the now-defunct *Stardust*, a Canadian sci-fi magazine, as well as *The Lost Moose Catalogue*, *Canadian Women's Studies*, *Kinesis*, *The Other Woman*, *The Pedestal,* and *The Open Door*.

Shelly Rafferty's recent work has appeared in *Queer View Mirror*, *Close Calls* (St. Martin's) and in *The Lesbian Review of Books*. Shelly writes about education and lives in a barn with her new baby, Jake.

Riddle lives, laughs, drinks, and does not drink coffee in Portland, Oregon.

Susan Fox Rogers is the editor of eight anthologies including *SportsDykes: Stories from On and Off the Field* and *Close Calls: New Lesbian Fiction*, and the author of *White Lies*, a young adult novel. She is working toward her MFA in creative non-fiction.

Meredith Rose used to milk cows for a living and now teaches English. Her stories appear in journals and zines and her chapbook of short-short stories *Lesbian Neurotica* is on sale now.

Rachel Rose has been published in *Fireweed*, *Prairie Fire*, *Arc*, *Calyx*, and *The Fiddlehead*. She was also awarded the 1997 Bronwen Wallace Prize. She is currently living in Quebec and completing a poetry manuscript, tentatively titled *Giving My Body To Science*, and a collection of short stories called *Want*.

Teresa Savage lives with her partner and their three children and earns money as a librarian. Her novella, *Vigia: an adventure in domesticity and desire,* will be published next year.

Delia Scales, after completing a post-graduate degree in art, turned to writing and has produced a novel and a number of short stories. She reads at fringe festivals, publishes in a range of magazines, and dreams of completing a detective story set in a women's refuge. Her story is an excerpt from a novel entitled *Invisible Web*.

Sarah Schulman is the author of nine books, most recently the novels *Shimmer* and *Rat Bohemia,* and the non-fiction books *Stagestruck: Theater, AIDS and Marketing* and *My American History: Lesbian and Gay Life During the Reagan/Bush Years.*

Anne Seale's tape of humorous love songs, *Sex for Breakfast*, is available from Wildwater Records, P.O. Box 56, Webster, NY 14580-0056. Other examples of Seale's work are found in the anthologies *Ex-lover Weird Shit, Love Shook My Heart, Pillow Talk*, and in issues of *Lesbian Short Fiction*.

Mercia Schoeman is a psychologist and lesbian activist. She lives in Durban, South Africa, with her lover and presents empowerment workshops in disadvantaged, rural schools of KwaZulu-Natal. She is currently the provinical convenor of the KwaZulu-Natal Coalition for Gay and Lesbian Equality.

Lori Shwydky is a writer living in Vancouver. She has published poetry, and written and produced several short films and videos. "Cherry Pie" is her first published short story. Lori is currently at work on her first feature-length screenplay.

Linda Smukler is the author of two collections of poetry: *Home in Three Days. Don't Wash*, which won the 1997 Firecracker Alternative Book Award in Poetry, and *Normal Sex*. She has received fellowships in poetry from the New York Foundation for the Arts and the Astraea Foundation and has also won the Katherine Anne Porter Prize in Short Fiction from *Nimrod* magazine.

Cecilia Tan is the author of *Black Feathers: Erotic Dreams* (HarperCollins) and *The Velderet* (Masquerade). Her short erotica has appeared in *Best American Erotica 1996* and *1998*, *Best Lesbian Erotica 1997*, and everywhere from *Penthouse* to *Ms.* magazine. She is the founder of Circlet Press, writes essays, and teaches erotic writing workshops.

Jules Torti lives in Ontario and has a fetish for women with blue hair wearing avocado green dresses. She hopes to arouse armchair nymphomaniacs everywhere with her work, making lesbians wet with words. Her work is to appear in the *Mammoth Book of Erotica* (Robinson), the *Seduction Anthology* (Alyson), and *Beginnings* (Alyson).

Kitty Tsui is the author of *Breathless* and *Sparks Fly* (writing as Eric Norton).

M. Anne Vespry (MAVerick) lives in Ottawa and tries to juggle feminism, studying law, dyke separatism, working on (dis)ability issues, authoring S/M smut, anti-racism from an interracial perspective, playing Dungeons and Dragons, anti-sizeism, colonizing cyberspace: the queer nerd frontier, and having enough time for her partner and dog.

Bonnie Waterstone is a full-time student living in New Westminster,

B.C. and interested in all aspects of writing. This piece marks her debut into lesbian fiction.

Jess Wells' seven volumes of work include a new anthology, *Lesbians Raising Sons*, and a novel, *AfterShocks,* which was nominated for an American Library Association Literary Award. Her four collections of short stories include *Two Willow Chairs* and *The Dress/The Sharda Stories*. Her work has appeared in more than twenty literary anthologies within the lesbian, gay, and women's movement.

Dianne Whelan lives on the Sunshine Coast of B.C. and is an award-winning photographer and part-time writer. She owns a publishing company, Lily Pad Productions Ltd., which publishes and distributes her photographs internationally.

Jeannie Witkin is a Jewish lesbian who transforms other people's words as a sign language interpreter. Writing lets her speak for herself. She has been published in *Queer View Mirror* and *Sinister Wisdom.*

Rita Wong lives in Vancouver. According to some sources, she turns butch upon crossing the American border. However, she would counter that she's neither butch nor femme whether she's down south or not. She is currently working on a manuscript of poems.

Tonya Yaremko lives in Vancouver with her partner Sharon and their four cats, Spirit, Amber, Mickey, and Mikey. Her work was published in *Queer View Mirror 2.*

ABOUT THE EDITOR

Karen X. Tulchinsky is the award-winning author of the short story collection *In Her Nature*. She co-edited *Queer View Mirror 1* and *2: Lesbian & Gay Short Short Fiction,* and *Tangled Sheets: Stories & Poems of Lesbian Lust,* and is the author of *Love Ruins Everything*, a novel. Karen co-wrote a piece that appeared in the Lambda Award-winning *Sister & Brother: Lesbians and Gay Men Talk About Their Lives Together*. She has written for numerous magazines including *Curve, Diva, The Georgia Straight, Look West*, and the *Lambda Book Report*. Karen lives, writes, and teaches creative writing in Vancouver.

Credits

"Her Thighs" was originally published in *Trash*, by Dorothy Allison, copyright © 1988, Firebrand Books, Ithaca, NY.

"History Lessons" was originally published in *Running Fiercely Toward a High Thin Sound*, by Judith Katz, copyright © 1992, Firebrand Books, Ithaca, NY.

"A Different Place" was originally published in *A Restricted Country* by Joan Nestle, copyright © 1987, Firebrand Books, Ithaca, NY.

"The Cutting" was originally published in *Breathless* by Kitty Tsui, copyright © 1996, Firebrand Books, Ithaca, NY.

"Beyond the Pale" was originally published in *Beyond the Pale,* by Elana Dykewomon, copyright © 1997, Press Gang Publishers, Vancouver, BC.

"Lemon Scent" was originally published in *Out On Main Street*, by Shani Mootoo, copyright © 1993, Press Gang Publishers, Vancouver, BC.

"People in Trouble" was originally published in *People in Trouble*, by Sarah Schulman, copyright © 1990, E.P. Dutton, New York, NY.

"Famous Last Words" was originally published as part of a story called "Women Who Make My Knees Weak," in *In Her Nature*, copyright © 1995 by Karen X. Tulchinsky, Women's Press, Toronto, and in *The Femme Mystique*, edited by Lesléa Newman, copyright © 1995, Alyson Publications, Los Angeles, CA.